In Praise of

I absolutely love this hot, steamy, captivating book with exceptional characters in an erotic world that is so realistic it felt like I was on the journey with them. I recommend reading this book by an extraordinary author that knows how to captivate the attention of their reader.

Kathleen -Booksprout Reviewer

Awesomely hot romance! Loved the characters and the story! Great chemistry! Hooked from the beginning!

Jen -Bookbub Reviewer

This is a slow-burn romance with scorching heat, you may need a few cold glasses of water. The story sucks you in and it kept me riveted. It's intense and sexy.

Marianela -Amazon Reviewer

I was completely addicted to the passion and chemistry between these characters!

Maggie -Amazon Reviewer

CASSIDY LONDON

Heatwave

International Love 3

Cassidy London
www.cassidylondon.com

CASSIDY LONDON

Copyright © 2020 Cassidy London Books

ALL RIGHTS RESERVED. This work is one of fiction. Any resemblance of the characters to persons living or deceased is purely coincidental. Names, places, and characters are figments of the author's imagination. All trademarked items included in this novel have been recognized as so by the author. The author holds exclusive rights to this work. Unauthorized duplication is prohibited.

ISBN: 978-1-7773017-2-9

Other Books by
CASSIDY LONDON

NEW ADULT ROMANCE TRILOGY
INTERNATIONAL LOVE SERIES

Freefall (#1) -Forbidden Love
Layover (#2) -Second Chance
Heatwave (#3) -Secret Billionaire

SEXY SMALL TOWN ROMANCE
MAPLE COVE SERIES

Falling In (#1) -Fake Fiancée
Books 2-3-4 -Coming Soon

ENEMIES TO LOVERS
STAND ALONE
Inked Love

SWINGERS ROMANCE NOVELLAS
SUBURBAN SECRETS SERIES

Couples Night Out (#1)
Weekend Getaway (#2)
Island Resort (#3)

CASSIDY LONDON

To finally letting go.

CASSIDY LONDON

Heatwave

International Love 3

CASSIDY LONDON

Prologue

New York

Samantha Jordan

He still tormented me in my dreams. The curl of his lip, the smell of his hot breath on my neck, those rough hands that roamed my body as he examined and took what he thought was his. I would listen to the click of the seconds on the clock as he catered to his own twisted needs. But with every minute that passed, the crevice in my soul deepened, slowly changing the course of my life forever.

Then again, maybe I was always meant for destruction.

After my parents died in a car crash when I was just eleven, it was Gammy, my great aunt, who took me in. She gave me a roof over my head and made sure I would have a solid future. She was an old lady with nothing more than the basics to offer, but she was all I had.

Gammy was of the mindset that the best place for children was church. She abhorred the secular lifestyle that her niece, my mother, had taken, and she was determined to turn me around. That meant private religious school, church, and a lot of stiff upper lip. She was relentless in her pursuit to change me. Unfortunately, I never made the cut and she seemed to relish in reminding me of that.

Never was that truer than when Father Dunberry offered to tutor me. I suppose in her eyes, being tutored by the priest was an honor. But it turned out to be a nightmare. It didn't take me long to realize what I had to do to improve my grades. When Dunberry's eyes roamed, my senses prickled, but when his hands roamed, I told Gammy.

At first, she accused me of lying, then of rebelling against her and being ungrateful. I never made mention of those awful tutoring sessions again.

Time went by and things did get better. Fortunately for me, Father Dunberry lost interest in my education as I aged. And of course, when he did, Gammy blamed me for it. As far as she was concerned, I had been damaged since birth. As if my mother getting pregnant at sixteen had somehow poisoned me.

When I hit my late teens, she found a new way to torture me. She shamed any kind of normal teenage behaviour, forcing me to retreat even further inside myself. Eventually, she no longer needed to use words. Her voice became a constant repeat in my head. She was forever reminding me that no matter where I went and what I did, I would never outrun my demons. That I would never reach my potential or surmount the demons of my past. That no matter how hard I tried, no one would ever love and accept me as I am because I, Samantha Jordan, was inherently damaged. A soul without purpose floating endlessly in a sea of ruin.

HEATWAVE

For years I tried to ignore it, to put those early years out of my head and live like they never happened. But eventually, sorrow seeped back in and latched on to every part of my world. It ate away at my trust, my self-confidence, and my ability to maintain relationships. So, I did what I could to survive. I shut the gate and lifted the drawbridge on all hopes of a normal life. I truly hoped to never feel anything again.

But that didn't mean I didn't crave the idea of being in love. I saw my friends fall in love, and time and time again, it left an unrequited longing in the depths of my soul. However, that wasn't the life for me. Mine was a solitary one, a life destined to remain alone.

After college, I threw myself into my work. Being a vet was my life. My love for animals had led me down the path to the local ER clinic. Despite massive student loans and dark circles under my eyes from too many overnight shifts, it filled me with purpose. Next to my post-grad internship in Australia, it was a great job.

But it was my post-grad internship year at the NSW Sydney Animal Clinic that had given me more than just experience in my field; it had healed my soul. Australia had somehow glued together the broken pieces of my life and enabled me to present myself to the world as a new person. A whole person. At least in public, anyway. After a year in Australia, I came back to the U.S. and, thanks to my internship, got a job at the NY Animal Urgent Care, a job I never would have had the experience for if not for Australia.

Now people knew me as Dr. Jordan, the vet who patched up their fur babies when they were sick or injured. I worked my ass off but I loved every second of it. Lately though, I had been distracted. It had been a little over a month since every news channel in America began filling up with images of Australia. The country, and specifically New South Wales, the area that I loved so much, was now in a state of emergency. This was no annual bush fire experience; Australia was burning, and it consumed me.

I had arrived in Australia more broken than I was even aware of, and somehow, the country and those tiny souls had saved me. I had always been drawn to animals. From the time I was a small child, I had felt a deep-seated connection to them. That feeling had guided almost every decision I had made over the course of my twenty-seven years. From the first stray cat that I took into my college dorm room, to my decision to become a vet, and every moment in between. Animals were where I found love. A giving, unconditional love that never hurt or betrayed me.

And now they were the ones who needed help. Even through the screen, I could see their fear and terror staring out and pleading for help. I knew that look. I knew it because I, too, had lived it. Not in the same way, but in one that evoked the same feelings. It was a brutal and paralyzing fear. One that was all consuming, that flooded every part of your being, leaving you with nowhere to find release. No respite from the pain that seared through every piece of flesh like a double-edged sword, the panic when it approached, and the pit of darkness that enveloped your life as it touched you.

Those cries of desperation and pain pounded into my head like a drill. I had to turn it off, make it stop. I told myself that I wouldn't do it anymore, continually pouring over every tidbit of information until I was nothing but a sniffling mess or scrolling past the endless articles filled with details about all the things that I couldn't change. It was killing me.

A part of my soul felt lost, knowing that it was happening and I was too far away to do anything about it. Of course, I had donated to the charities, reached out to friends and acquaintances that still lived there, but I wished that there was more I could do. As much as I wanted to drop everything at home and rush to Australia's aid, I couldn't leave my job. I lived in a shitty shoebox apartment, ate Ramen most nights, and had so much student debt that I was already on a lifetime payback plan.

If I could've avoided social media, I might have been okay. But I couldn't. I was drawn to it to like a moth to a flame, soaking up every last horrific image and letting it eat away at my soul. Like an addict slowly sinking deeper, I could feel them calling for me and I didn't know how to answer.

Minutes would turn to hours as time disappeared into a constant scrolling and clicking of links. I stared and poured over every piece of information. The statistics, the weeks, the fires, the animals. Talks of extinction and irreparable damage. With each word, I was ripped apart again and again. The place that had saved me and that had given me a new life when I had none was now in peril. I was granted a new purpose and way to bear my cross and step out into the world each day.

The only problem was that the more I let myself feel their pain, the faster I would begin to remember my own.

Samantha Jordan.

My name. Drawn out of the depths, like the dark cackle of her laugh.

Stop acting like a spoiled baby.

Forever mocking and poking the bear that tried desperately to eternally sleep.

What do you think you're going to do? You have nothing to offer. Remember where you came from.

She often spoke to me like that. But I couldn't blame her, not really. She was the voice that brought me back to reality, the cruel words that played on repeat in my head. Never letting me forget that it was all my fault.

Although the hot sun of Australia had healed my surface wounds, nothing could ever take away the deep hidden scars. They bound me and held me together because without them, I didn't exist. So, along with the rest of the world, I watched Australia burn, silently swallowing back tears that never made it to the surface.

HEATWAVE

London

Ashton Chase

Time had passed, but I remembered it like it was yesterday. Visions of those last brutal moments before the darkness hit would fill my mind, smoke filling my lungs and bile rising in my stomach. It came to me every time I turned on the faucet. With my hands on the cold tiles, I would try to absorb the hot water as it poured over my naked flesh, fighting desperately to let it soothe me. It never did. Somehow, from the depths of my mind, the unmistakable scent of burning flesh would fill the air and imprison me in my tiled cell.

Lost in the haze of my own mind, the soap slipped, jolting me from my vision with a clatter on the tiles. The smoky mist somehow evaporated back into my mind and all that was left was the scent of jasmine shampoo. My nose wrinkled in disgust. Far too flowery for my liking. I would have to let Sylvia know to switch it. Smelled like a woman, and that was the last thing I needed. Betrayal is a funny thing. It hardens you. Makes you turn away despite the constant longing.

At first, being a firefighter had come naturally to me. It was a calling that healed the broken pieces. Finally, being the one to save instead of being saved gave me purpose and fulfillment. Until that day when I heard a child crying behind the rubble. I tried and tried but just couldn't reach him. Old wounds were opened and panic set in. My mission was aborted and my team took over. Just as quickly as they pulled me out of the fire, my control fell apart. Life doled out yet another beating as I lost the career and the woman I loved all at the same time.

After that, I had to begin again. This process wasn't new to me, though. I had always been the master of reinvention. I soon realized that if I couldn't save people's lives or the ones they loved, then I would save the next best thing; their money.

Stepping out of the shower, I wrapped a fluffy white towel around my waist and contemplated my reflection in the mirror. The circles under my eyes had become darker, and signs of age seemed to be showing more than usual. At thirty-five years old, I felt like I had lived a lifetime and then some.

I dried off quickly and headed back down the hall to my room. My flat was a penthouse suite over-looking the Thames. It still blew my mind that I lived there. From my abusive beginnings in a run-down farmhouse to a happy suburban foster family was already quite the jump. But from poverty to a life of luxury, well, it was simply unheard of where I came from.

Glancing at the time, I made haste. Time was ticking and if I dawdled any longer, I would miss out on the action. The market opened in ten minutes and I needed to do my job.

Managing other people's money and playing the stock market had started as a hobby after I left the station. But right from the start, it was an easy game for me to own. I had spent my life playing games, and although my life started out filled with shit, the games that I was forced to play taught me to read people and situations like no one else. Soon, friends starting seeing the success I was having and asked me to help them out and it just took off from there.

HEATWAVE

In the space of just a few years, I was managing the portfolios of London's elite. High society, celebrities, and even some dukes and counts were amongst my clients. They had made me wealthier than I ever thought possible. Friends recommended me, and my circle grew as did my client base. Before I knew it, I had become one of the UK's top financial managers and stock brokers. Head-hunters and firms started knocking on my door, but that wasn't the life for me.

My therapist at the time hadn't supported it. I was supposed to be resting and healing he said. It wasn't the time for a new career when I had barely healed from the devastating effects of the last one. Only fighting fires hadn't been a career, it had been a calling. A calling to save and protect the way others had once saved me. The firemen had seemed invincible that night. Like superheroes, tearing down the walls to get to me. Such a child-like perspective. But they were only human and if their mission had failed...I knew what the outcome would have been. Because, it wasn't just that moment or that fire. My first memory and all the ones thereafter had been filled with the terror that my father inflicted on our family. If the fire hadn't consumed me that night in the shed, it would have been the next time or the one after that. Dad would have made sure of it.

But that was all behind me now and I had finally learned to put myself first. My life was set, certain, and predictable. My days of getting into the flames were over. I had accepted that years ago. But why did I still have this nagging feeling that change was coming again?

Maybe it was the current state of the world. The new year had started off with tragedy. Australia was impossible to ignore. It was splashed all over every screen day in and day out. It was wreaking havoc on a beautiful country and having affects world-wide.

I could see it across my screen, the fear and desperation. It was in the eyes of the Australian people who were fleeing their own homes and helping their neighbors to evacuate. But there was also hope. Hope when they reached a safe area and opened their arms to hold each other. I saw the gratitude in their eyes when they took the hands of those who helped. I even saw it in the eyes of the animals who were carried out of the wreckage and into the vet clinics. And who was amidst all this chaos? My kin. The men and women of the fire brigade. The ones who were first on the scene and last to leave. The family I used to belong to. Despite being in London and so far removed from that tragedy, when I saw the firefighters on screen, it was like looking into the eyes of my own team.

It had killed my soul to leave my guys. Even now, when I squeezed my eyes shut, I could still remember that last time, minutes before the panic set in, and the realization that it might be my last time.

Someone I loved once told me that my worst quality was my extremism. She said it as a way to shame me, but actually, I've since found that it is the only thing that serves me well. When she betrayed me with one of my buddies during my recovery, a time when I had needed her the most, my reaction might have seemed extreme to some.

HEATWAVE

As soon as I had found out, I packed up all her things and moved her out of my flat without so much as a conversation. When I was no longer permitted to fight fires, I turned on a dime and started a new career. I can always count on being extreme when things fall apart.

The same feeling consumed me when I thought of Australia. Once I knew that I couldn't sit on the sidelines any longer, I made my move. It took me less than a week to pack up my life, get on a plane, and settle in NSW. I secured temporary homes for my animals with friends and neighbors, then called up my team and ensured that they could take over the bulk of my work while I was away. It was a bold move, and one that everyone was telling me would cost me my business. Yet, somehow following my heart was never the hard thing to do.

Chapter 1

New York

Samantha Jordan

The sound of my phone jolted me out of a deep slumber. That incessant beeping still drove me crazy even after all this time. Loud, aggressive, and relentless in its pursuit of my attention, which is what it was looking for in that moment. Somewhere inside my subconscious, I was floating above the clouds, looking down on the earth.

"Dr. Jordan." I answered as I cleared my throat, trying to remove the sound of sleep despite it being 3am.

"We need you down in the ER."

"Be there in twenty minutes." I mumbled, despite knowing that time frame was too long. When they called at this hour, it was because I needed to hustle my ass out the door. With barely a second to brush the cobwebs from my mind, I jumped out of bed and began pulling on my scrubs and my favorite grey sweatshirt with the words 'NY Animal Urgent Care' across the middle. A trip to the bathroom and a quick teeth-brushing happened before my hand grabbed the pre-packed bag that I kept by the door. There was certainly nothing glamorous about being an emergency vet. It was a no make-up, no fuss type of job and most of the time, that suited me just fine. I had it down to a fine art.

Glancing at my Apple watch as the front door slammed behind me, my mind filled with the possibilities of what could be happening. Messages and emails were popping up like wildfire, but there was no time for that. The elevator in my building was slow at this time of night, so I bolted down the stairs instead. I always found that the quick jog kept my adrenaline pumping and my mind focused.

I glanced at my watch again. A summary popped up. Three dogs with chocolate poisoning, a dog fight victim, and the reason they woke me…a police dog from the local K9 unit who was shot in the line of duty. It was going to be a long shift. Typically, I chose to stay on call at the hospital and sleep in one of the dorms. But it had been slow earlier that evening and there were enough vets that I took the opportunity to go home for some creature comforts. Fuck. Never should have.

Fortunately, 3am driving was pretty easy and I made it to the emergency room in less time than I expected. Despite the difficulty of seeing animals in pain, I loved my job. I had always had an affinity for animals, ever since I was a young child. Animals, even the ones who weren't friendly, had unconditional love hard wired into their furry little brains. They possessed a quality that humans didn't. My kinship with them was cosmic and I had always felt it was my duty to be their advocate.

"Dr. Jordan, you're here!" called out Julia, the receptionist on duty, as I flew through the door. "Did you get the updates?"

"Sure did!" I called back with a smile as I pulled my long brown hair back into a ponytail.

HEATWAVE

"It's go time!" I threw my sweatshirt and bag over the desk to her. There was no time to make it to my locker and back again. Julia was used to my dedication, though. Many other vets would have checked themselves in at a leisurely pace, but being an emergency vet meant more to me than just a job. It was my life, my identity.

"Isn't it always around here?" I heard Julia call back as I kept running down the hall.

Flinging the swinging doors open, I burst into the surgery prep room. The stench of blood and sanitizer filled my nostrils. I should have been used to it by now, yet it always made my stomach turn a little. My eyes fixed on the center of the room. On the gurney was a beautiful German Shepard named Drake, his large girth masked under a sheet, and only his head visible from the top. On his face was an oxygen mask. He was still; sedated. The nurses and techs were already giving me the rundown of his injuries. He'd been hit in his hind flank and although he was strong, the prognosis wasn't great. He'd lost a ton of blood and the bullet was lodged in a difficult place. Had he been a house pet, his people would have been counseled to let him go. But his owner was a cop, and because Drake was close to retirement, his owner pleaded for us to at least try. Even though he'd never return to his former glory, he deserved to finish off his life with the family he loved. I could only hope that I would be able to do enough for him.

I finished drying off my hands as a technician pulled the scrubs over my arms. Taking my place by the gurney, I took a second for a silent prayer. I never prayed, but somehow my Catholic school upbringing always seemed to surface right before a surgery.

***

Four hours later, I collapsed on the couch in the staff room.

"You look like you need an espresso, Sam. Or maybe a few." Chuckled Ann-Marie, a fellow vet who sported a bright red bob straight from a box of cheap hair color. She was a bit quirky, but truly a sweetheart and someone who had become a good friend since we began working together.

"Shit, who doesn't around here? Especially after surgery." I answered.

"Well, you're shit out of luck my friend, because all we have is this crappy, lukewarm coffee." She answered, holding out a mug.

"The way I'm feeling, I'll take it anyway." I laughed, as I stood up to reach for the mug. Although it wasn't as hot as I would have liked, I wrapped my hands around the base and relaxed into it, letting the warmth travel into my hands and up my arms. Returning to my spot on the lumpy, worn out couch, I flicked on the television to my favorite news channel.

"Anything different?" Ann-Marie asked, grabbing a seat on the couch next to me.

"I wish…" I answered under my breath. Watching the news was becoming an obsessive and paralyzing issue for me. It had been over a month and other than work, it was all I could think of.

Watching images of fire ravaged land, displaced people, and singed animals broke my heart. Everyone, of course, was saddened by the on-screen horrors. But having lived there for a year somehow made me feel like, in some way, it was my home, too.

"Samantha!" The sound of my name jolted me out of my sadness. My head turned as I heard a familiar voice calling my name. *Fuck.* It was Dave. Dr. Dave Jeffries, a colleague and long-time acquaintance from back in school. My skin prickled with uneasiness as he waltzed in to the room and stood, feet spread, hands on his waist, and a slimy grin plastered across his face.

"Hey Dave." Ann-Marie answered. I just nodded my head and sipped my lukewarm, bitter coffee.

"Heard you saved the police dog, Sam."

I nodded. Getting into a conversation with Dave was never a good thing. No matter what I said or didn't say, it always seemed to lead him on. I'd been told I had that effect on men. I didn't see it, but Gammy did. She always said I needed to be more low-key. Somehow, just my presence seemed to attract men. Even if she hadn't drilled that into my head since the day my breasts grew in, Father Dunberry definitely confirmed it for me. Old habits were hard to break.

27

I shuddered at the memories. They always appeared and took me by surprise in the worst possible moments.

Or maybe Dave just liked a challenge? Whatever the case, I tried to keep my distance from him. His persistence and slimy demeanour gave me the creeps. But I also had to work with him, so I tried to keep it civil, too. It was a constant balancing act that never seemed to be resolved.

Dave wasn't the kind of guy to give up, though. He seemed to sense my hesitation and take it as me trying to play hard-to-get. Other girls didn't seem to see what I did either. Where I saw a slimy personality and small black beady eyes, others saw charm.

Anyway, it didn't matter. Even if he hadn't rubbed me the wrong way, the fact was, I didn't date. I didn't hook up. I didn't anything. Not anymore anyway. I'd tried during college and in the years after, but it had never worked. If I didn't get annoyed with their shenanigans, I eventually had that same uncontrollable panic attack that scared them off. I no longer bothered. I was twenty-seven years old and destined to be alone forever. But it was okay. I preferred it that way.

I needed to make my move and do it quickly. Jumping up from the couch, I pushed past Dave, made my way to the sink, and dumped out the rest of my coffee.
"I have to go, guys. Need to take care of a few things." My voice squeaked a little too high as it always did when I was nervous. Walking with conviction, I made my way to the door without looking back. Out in the hall, I picked up speed.

"Sam, wait up!" Dave called as he ran down the hall towards me. I stopped in my tracks, hesitating before I turned. When I did, it was his bright smile and hopeful eyes that made me dread his next words.

"Dave, I'm exhausted just coming off a brutal surgery. Please. I need to get my shit together and rest before my next shift starts."

"I know, I know." He said as he wrapped an arm around me, making me shudder internally. It always felt as though he had an ulterior motive. And I was positive that it involved me being naked.

"It's just that I saw this and thought of you." He continued, handing me a paper.

I opened it slowly, the pit of my stomach already sending me warning signals. God, I hoped it wasn't a love note. I didn't have the ability to stomach him professing his love to me at this time. But as I unfolded the paper, my heart began to race for a different reason. First came the logo of the NSW Sydney Animal Clinic. I smiled, remembering the best year of my life.

"Want to apply? We could do it together," Dave asked, an eerie calm smile spreading across his face. "I remember you saying how much you loved it there. And now with all the fires, this is a great way to help!" I noticed how he stared at my breasts as he spoke to me. It was as if his words said one thing, but his eyes clearly said another.

"You see, Samantha, he's not interested in you, he just wants what you're flaunting. You know what he wants and we all know that you're going to give it to him."

She never let up. I pushed Gammy to the back of my mind and shut the door on the voice's incessant chattering.

"Wow, thanks for thinking of me, Dave. I really do appreciate it. But, umm…well, I really can't afford to take a leave from work. I have too many debts. You should apply, though." I responded hopefully. Maybe this would get rid of him for a while.

"Well, here's the thing, Sam. Our clinic will fund the trip. Although it's volunteer and there's no salary, everything would be paid for by our clinic. Obviously, the work would be different, probably harder and longer hours, but…"

I felt as though I would self-combust. It wasn't possible. Was this a real opportunity? Grabbing the papers back from Dave, I scanned it again.

"There's just one little thing, honey." Dave paused, his fingers running the length of my arm. "They require two vets."

His black beady eyes stared right through me.

"We're the perfect match. We're both great at our jobs. What do you say? You, me, and a few months in Australia."

I sucked in air and grounded myself to the floor.

"Dave. It says here that you need experience with Australian animals. This is not just any call for volunteers. You don't have that kind of experience."

"Well, I figured you could call them up and give me a stellar recommendation." He slowly exhaled. "And in return, I'll help you with some of those student debts." His hand curled around mine, holding it tight.

Bile crept up the back of my throat, but I swallowed it down and forced a smile to my lips.
"I'll think about it." I answered, pulling back my hand and stuffing the letter in my purse.

"Sorry, Dave, I really have to go." I muttered, slowly backing away.

"I'll leave it in your hands then, sweetheart." He winked back at me.

God, that man made me want to swallow my own puke.

Chapter 2

Australia

Ashton Chase

Ambien was always my in-flight go-to, but as soon as the wheels touched down, my eyes shot open and my chemical induced slumber was gone as quickly as it came. Shaking off the groggy remains, I chugged back the rest of my water and began gathering my things.

For a moment or two, doubt seeped in. My life was easy now. I had a successful career, a life of luxury, friends and clients who respected me, not to mention all the sex money could buy. Gone was that little boy from the burning shed, the one who constantly needed to prove he was worth saving by running into fires to save others. Yet here I was. Five years since the panic attack that ruined my career, touching down on the Australian coast in the middle of the worst bushfire season of my generation. What had made me leave the safety and familiarity of my secure lifestyle? Images of displaced injured animals and children running for their lives while the flames burned around them. It had struck a chord in me that I just couldn't ignore any longer. I hadn't seen it coming, but extreme decisions were what I was made of. I had to follow my gut.

Opening my phone, I quickly connected to Wi-Fi and sent a message to my pre-booked Uber. I began counting my timeline backwards. Inside the Air BnB, Uber ride, luggage pickup, customs. List making and time scheduling had always helped to keep my demons at bay.

It was all about keeping my mind occupied so it didn't self-combust. I did with work, too. I had memorized all the numbers in each of my client's investment portfolios. Knowing the details like the back of my hand, and being able to recite or count them down, grounded me. It kept me focused, in control, and solid. I realized it was something that I had always done when the therapist I was seeing after my panic attack pointed it out to me. I had let my emotions get the better of me that night. Everything seemed to be better when I focused on controlling the little things around me. I had learned that for the first time when, at five years old, I was convinced that I was facing certain death. When it seems like the world is caving in, you do what you know, and I could feel the details of a minute task burning in my mind. I could count the lines on tree bark as well as I could count numbers. The more details the better. Had I just focused on the job and used my own coping mechanisms, my last night as a firefighter might have turned out differently. Too late for that moment, but I would never forget again.

Customs, luggage pick up, and all that jazz was better than I had expected and before I knew it, I was standing outside in the burning hot sun.

My Uber pulled up and the driver opened the window and called out, "You Ashton Chase, mate?"

"Yep! That's me! Right here!" I called back as I approached the car. The A/C inside was a welcome relief from the sweltering heat. Even in the few minutes that I had stood outside, I was already sweating. Such a change from the perpetual dampness of London.

Thankfully, the driver wasn't a chatty guy and I was able to relax and take in the scenery as we drove. At first, it was like any other drive. But before long, the sky turned gray and the landscape began to turn from lush to desecrated. Black ash covered the ground, homes and landscapes burned to the ground; an apocalyptic landscape that I had only seen on a film screen. The lump in my throat seemed to double in size as I swallowed it back down. Leaning my head back on the headrest, I closed my eyes and took a deep breath. I then opened my phone and began to review the last numbers my team had sent me.

A little over an hour later and I was finally on the couch inside the cool air of the Air BnB, a beer in my hand and my laptop open. Almost all was right in my world. I made a call to my friend Bradley to let him know I had arrived. Bradley was a good guy. We had worked together back in London in the fire brigade and he had been one of my closest friends at the time. Although we had each gone different ways since then, when we spoke, it was as if time hadn't passed.

Looking around, I felt comfortable in the condo. It was Bradley's beachfront place that faced Bondi Beach. He usually rented it out this time of year, except the tourists weren't coming this season. Light, airy, and decorated mostly in white, it was everything that was expected of a beachfront condo. Despite my luxurious lifestyle, I was a simple man. Other than the necessities, all I needed was my laptop. I had only told my clients that I would be travelling for a while and my team was taking over their accounts. The truth wasn't their business.

Some would have been less than thrilled and might have even moved their money elsewhere if they knew that I was going halfway across the world to volunteer as a firefighter in some of the worst bushfires this country had ever seen. They wouldn't have understood, and more importantly, they wouldn't have cared. Not all of them, but there was definitely a large percentage of people I dealt with that only cared about one thing; their money. Regardless, I wouldn't let them down. I opened my laptop and logged in to check out the state of their affairs.

Despite my often-conflicted feelings about the ultra-rich, these people were the reason I was following my gut. A London firefighter's salary would never have taken me here. Plus, if I was still at the station, I might be shackled in an unhappy relationship and maybe even with kids by now. I shuddered at the memories. Olivia had been my life. And I had thought she always would be. Until I found naked pictures on her phone with another man while I was recovering from a mental breakdown. I still had the images of her screaming in the street when she found her things and I had changed the locks. The bitch. She had the nerve to tell me she loved me after what she did. At least I had found out before I asked her to marry me.

Women were just like my mother. She had never protected me from my dad. She let it all happen and then cried and told me she loved me. She was pathetic. And so was Olivia. When shit got difficult and I was sick, she went off with my friend, and then cried and said she was sorry and really did love me.

HEATWAVE

It took me a long time to get over Olivia's betrayal. By the time I did, the station was far away in my past, and the only women in my circle were more interested in where my bank account could take them on vacation than anything about my life. Shallow, materialistic, and just like Olivia, doling out betrayal left, right, and center. They sold their pussies to the highest bidders and relished in their winnings on the yachts of the men who entrusted their savings to me.

Maybe it was me, maybe I had never truly understood women. Maybe I didn't even want to anymore.

After a second swig of beer, I pulled out my phone to text Bradley.

Hey mate, I made it. Settling in now. Let me know when you want to come by. Looking forward to hearing about how I can help you guys out.

With that, I turned my attention back to my spreadsheets, and dove into playing catch up on some work.

CASSIDY LONDON

Chapter 3

New York

Samantha Jordan

I lay on the tiny cot in the staff room, staring at the ceiling and hoping for a sign. My heart had skipped a beat when I first read the letter. It was everything I wanted to be doing. Heading out into some of the most badly affected areas and saving the poor babies who were clinging to the trees in terror, providing love and care and medical attention, saving lives that never should have been disrupted. Yes, the animals needed my help here, but my foster country was burning and they didn't have enough help.

The only thing that had me hesitating was the Dave issue. If not for him, I might not have known about this opportunity. Yet, there was no way in hell I'd be going anywhere with Dave. I could barely be in the same room as him. How did he not see it?

Uncomfortable though it was, it was manageable to keep him at bay at work. However, there was no way I was going to recommend him. But the program required a pair…I chewed my nails trying to figure out a way around it.

I would certainly be thrilled to not have his roaming eyes all over me. Ugh. Just the thought of him made me recoil inside my own skin. However, if I was accepted, which honestly, the more I read the requirements, the more I knew this was the path I needed to take, I could keep my job and help the country that I loved so much.

There was also the issue of money. They would take care of the trip and I'd be given housing on site, but this was volunteer work and it meant I'd be missing out on the paycheck I had worked my ass off to get. Plus, with all the debt I had accumulated…well, it wasn't an easy choice.

As I lay in the dark on the tiny cot, I weighed the pros and cons. Minutes ticked by and then, as if I had already known all along, I jumped up from the bed and grabbed my phone.
Filling out the online application took less than five minutes. In the comments section, I explained that despite not having a partner, I didn't need one. I had lived and worked in Australia before and specifically, at the NSW Sydney Animal Clinic. I was well acquainted with everything. Maybe the universe would shine down on me and make this work.

Just before I pressed send, I paused…but then…FUCK IT. I didn't owe him anything. Okay, maybe I did, but I was choosing to ignore that part. I'd tell him that I recommended him as well. *Maybe. Maybe not.*

Setting my alarm, I rolled over in an attempt to find some peace. Normally, a coffee would have prevented me from even closing my eyes, but the staff room java was about as potent as apple juice. My mind drifted in and out of consciousness and soon settled into a darkness that brought me some comfort.

I wasn't sure how long I had slept when my body sat up, jolting me awake unexpectedly. The room was still pitch black but my heart was racing. Images of flames surrounding me was still vivid in my mind. Drenched in sweat, I reached around frantically for my phone. I needed light. I needed to know the time. How long had I slept? What time was it? Why didn't my alarm go off? Why didn't anyone wake me?

Finally, I found it lodged beneath my leg. Pulling it out and squinting into the screen, I was shocked with what I saw. Three hours? Shit. I guess I had been more exhausted than I thought. I wondered if anyone realized I was still at the hospital.

Ding.

My email started downloading. NSW flashed across the screen. My heart skipped a beat. It couldn't be. Could it? Maybe it was an automatic response. There's no way they would have emailed me back so quickly.

I quickly opened my email and scanned past numerous spam messages until I saw the one that called my name.

Dear Dr. Jordan,

Thank you for reaching out and responding to our call for help. We have been made aware of the fabulous work you did during your internship at the NSW Sydney Animal Clinic during your internship, and we would be honoured that you are considering offering your services to help out the relief project.

As you know, this is typically a call for two vets as there is a housing shortage. However, we have another vet in the same situation who we could house you with if you agree to live together.

You'll find this information attached.

Please confirm with us asap if you will be joining us and when.

With much gratitude,

Dr. Joel Watson
Director of Emergency Services
NSW Sydney Animal Clinic

My throat closed up as I read and tears began to fill my eyes. This was my calling, proof that everything in life does come full circle, my reason for being. I needed to move quickly.

After quickly typing back a response, I pulled my sweater over my head and grabbed all my belongings out of my locker. My mind was in a daze as I zipped down the hall towards the elevator, already thinking of packing up my apartment, the things I needed to bring, and who I needed to contact. There wasn't much, really. Being that this wasn't the first time I'd thought about leaving, I already had tentative plans in place. I had just needed the catalyst to get there.

A part of me did feel bad about Dave. Just a few hours after he had brought this opportunity to my attention, I had secured it for myself and was making my plans to leave. Other than guilt about being an awful bitch, the upside was that maybe he would hate me after this. I could only hope…

Whatever, I had no time to think about him. I had more important things to focus on. He'd get over it. Besides, if he really wanted to go, he would have found a way. This had all been about him getting the opportunity to be my roommate. Ugh. I shuddered at the thought. He was an accomplished doctor in his own right. He certainly didn't need me to open doors for him. And besides, I justified in my mind, his reasons weren't in the right place. He didn't give a shit about the cause. Dave wanting to go to Australia was less about helping out the wildlife and more about having me all to himself on a trip. *Not happening, Dave. Not now, not ever.*

The elevator beeped as it reached the fourth floor. I marched down the hall to our scheduling coordinator, Brianna's, office. I knocked purposefully on her closed door.

"Come in." Called Brianna from the other side.

I took a deep breath and pushed the door open to find Brianna standing at her filing cabinet.

"Hi, Brianna!" I began brightly. "I hate to drop in unannounced, but I really need to talk to you."

"Hey, Dr. Jordan!" She responded, her warm smile easing my nerves slightly. "No worries, just give me a second to file these documents." She continued as she turned her back to drop the files into the cabinet.

The few seconds it took Brianna to settle herself gave me the time to breathe deeply and hone in on why I was doing this. I knew this would come as a surprise to my colleagues, especially as many of them didn't know about my internship or love for Australia.

"So, when will you leave?" She asked earnestly after I had gotten her up to speed.

"And just so you know, Sam…I'm so proud of you. Honestly, too many people just sit by and watch a disaster unfold. Not many ever pick up and head right in. Myself included. So, know how much I admire you for doing this."

"Thanks, I guess…" Brianna's words, although heartfelt, made me feel awkward. This wasn't about impressing people, it was about going where my heart called. I've always lived by the idea that when you see a sign, you go for it. Don't explain it or justify it, just do it. And strangely enough, this gift had been given to me by the person I disliked the most.
I wasn't sure what that sign meant.

As I left Brianna's office and made my way back down the hallways and towards the main entrance, I mentally counted items to pack as I marched. I heard my name being called once again. I turned my head to see Dave running after me for the second time that night. Once again, a cold shiver crept up my back, making the hairs on my neck stand on end.

I raised my hands, "Dave, please" I began, ready to explain my actions.

I never even had the chance, though. Hands connected with the nape of my neck, and spun me around. In an instant, the full force of his body pushed against mine. I felt myself slam back into the cement wall, my molars crashing together and reverberating inside my skull.

"What the fuck is your problem?" He snarled into my face. His hot breath blanketed my senses, setting off every alarm bell in my head.

"I've been nothing but nice to you and this is how you screw me over?"

Shit. How did he even know? Trembling, I attempted to find my voice. "I...I'm sorry, Dave. I...I...please, you're hurting me. Get off of me!" I shoved and pushed my hands into his chest, twisting my face away from his as I tried to get a hold on my unravelling emotions.

"Sam! Sam!" I heard Brianna's voice in the distance.

Dave growled under his breath but took a step back. "It's not over between us, Samantha." He stated, his eyes dark and sinister.

Brianna came running up and wrapped an arm around Dave's shoulder. "Oh Sam, I was just telling Dave about your news! Sorry if I let the cat out of the bag, but it's just so exciting!" She gushed.

"Yeah…um…it's fine, Bri." I mumbled, still trying to fix the hair that had fallen out of my ponytail when Dave accosted me.

A calmness overtook Dave's face as he announced. "It's really exciting, Samantha. I'm just so happy for you. Can't wait to hear about all the great work you'll be doing over there."

It was even creepier to see the transformation from aggressive to calm. His face changed in an instant. All of a sudden, he was the picture of peace and friendship.

"Here, Sam." Brianna continued as she shoved papers into my shaking hands. "You'll need these for your file. If you could just get all this taken care of before you go that would great."

"Of course, Bri. Not a problem." I answered, inhaling sharply and trying to get my bearings.

Just then Dave stepped forward and wrapped an arm around my torso, instantly hugging me to his body and holding me tight. "So proud of this girl! Always ready to help!"

To my dismay, Brianna actually winked at me and started to back away. "I think I'll go now…" Dave was making it look like the situation was something else and she was falling for it. To my horror, he grinned a slow, calculated grin and tipped an imaginary hat to Brianna as she backed away.

My escape window was closing in on me. "Yeah, I have to go, too. Sorry!" I said loudly so Brianna would hear me. I slipped from Dave's grip and ran down the hall after Brianna.

Shit. Not much had changed since childhood. Why did these creeps always find me? The kind of men who had everyone fooled. But I had only been fooled once. Never again.

Brianna and I moved quickly down the hall and away from Dave. I was acutely aware of him staring at us as we walked away. It was only when we turned the corner and I saw the front door that I felt relief.

Chapter 4

Australia

Ashton Chase

Standing on the balcony, I inhaled deeply and tried to pause the moment in an effort to appreciate what was right in front of me. The view was incredible. Bradley's condo was just a short walking distance to Bondi Beach. I could see the famous spot from his front porch and it was beautiful. The light sparkled off the clear water and within minutes, the warmth of the sun's rays were burning a hole in my skin.

To the right, dark grey clouds on the periphery of the picture-perfect view reminded me of the devastation and destruction that were nothing more than a short driving distance away. The fires weighed on my mind as did my work.

Despite having my team cover me, I was still wary about it all. It was going to be a challenge managing my client's needs while fighting fires on Bradley's team. I didn't want to disappoint either, so I would have to be smart about it. The time difference was on my side, though. I would have to forgo sleeping, but there were worse things in life. I was determined to make it work. And I had a backup plan. If things got too out of hand and I couldn't handle both, I was prepared to call in even more reinforcements from back home.

The one thing I didn't want to do was reveal to the guys at the station too many details about my life. In the first few years that I spent building my business, my circle was still very much station guys, and the more success I found, the more our friendships deteriorated. I was no longer one of the guys. They seemed to see me as a larger than life character who no longer fit in their circles. Maybe they resented my success or maybe they just couldn't relate anymore, I don't know. But either way, I lost the only family I'd ever had. Definitely didn't want to deal with that type of bullshit now. I had already planned out my story, and fortunately Bradley, who was one of the few fire station guys who I was still in touch with, was in on it.

But in the meantime, I had some time and needed to put it to good use. A few hours buying and selling, along with updates of portfolios, and I was ready to tackle my second most important task. The gym. Fortunately, this condo had one of its own. My cover was that of a fitness trainer, so I needed to look the part. This wasn't too difficult, though. Working out was something that I loved to do. I knew fighting fires was a physically demanding job, not to mention the mental strain of heading outside each day, and for that I had to stay focused. I'd been told that I didn't fit the image of a financial guy, but working out as hard as I did definitely helped me focus. As for the mental training, well, fitness helped with that, too.

I changed out of my clothes and slipped into a pair of dark grey gym shorts and a white tank top, laced up my tennis shoes, and made my way to the private gym. Bradley's place even had a pool inside the private garden in the back. I'd been doing the same routine for years. Cardio, free weights, and a swim.

HEATWAVE

I'd start out with what I knew, but I could see myself taking my run to the beach next time.

Chugging half the water that I had grabbed from the kitchen, I hopped onto the treadmill and set it for medium speed. I could easily bang out 6.5 miles in about thirty minutes. I'd been running since my teens when it was the only way to stop the madness encroaching in my head. As the sweat began to pour out of me, my mind cleared, and I focused on the weights I'd be doing next. I knew that in order to use the hose and carry items, or even the injured, I would need both upper body strength and solid hip and leg strength. Arms, chest, and thighs were no longer just for aesthetics, they were essential.

Bradley had told me what I'd be doing. Even though I was coming in as a volunteer, he was assigning me as if I was a full member of his team. And since I wasn't planning on reveling my current career or identity to these guys, I'd have to be able to hold my own no matter what. I had asked Bradley to back me up with my fitness instructor and part-time volunteer fireman from London routine. I just had to be able to play the part as well.

CASSIDY LONDON

Chapter 5

San Francisco

Samantha Jordan

Traveling to Australia the second time around seemed to be longer than the first. And I had only completed the first of two flights. Maybe that was because the first time I didn't know what to expect. Or maybe it was because I was filled with hopes and dreams about a fairy tale existence, far removed from the memories of the past. Getting lost in my head was one of my specialties, and I remembered dreaming about falling in love on the gold coast and surfing during my time off from being a successful veterinarian. I had thought I'd stay there long after my internship ended. But life never seemed to work the way I planned it to.

After college, I'd been in debt up to my eyeballs, and everywhere I turned there were expectations of me. My professors wanted me to continue on and offered me positions in their research labs. My co-workers at the NSW hospital wanted me to stay on with them. My best friends, Ava and Adriana, encouraged me to visit them around the world as they lived their own lives. As for me, I felt lost. Gammy had left me nothing in her will. Not that I should have been surprised. She left it all to the church that had almost killed my spirit.

So, in the end, I opted for that which would help me pay off my bills. Despite the scholarship I had received, college was a killer, and I knew I'd have to work for years before being debt free. So I took the jobs that paid the most and ended up stateside once more.

And now here I was, not long after making those so-called smart decisions, still an exorbitant amount of debt to deal with, back on a flight that would get me to Australia. Choosing the right path was meaningless unless it's what you really wanted, I suppose.

My layover was in San Francisco and that suited me well because my friend Adriana was based there. Adri and I were old college friends. We used to be a group of three with Ava, but as inseparable as we had been back in the day, it had been years since we had seen each other in person.

Thankfully, social media kept us in touch, if you could even call it that. That was more Adri's style. I wasn't one to post or even scroll incessantly. However, we hadn't seen each other since Ava's wedding three years earlier and I owed her a dinner if nothing else. Fortunately, Adriana was a flight attendant and the airport was literally her second home, or maybe her first. We planned to meet for drinks and dinner during my four-hour layover at SFO.

"Sam!!" I heard Adri screech my name as she came barrelling into me, wrapping her arms around my waist and pulling me into a long-awaited hug. I giggled as she held me tight. Emotion welled up inside me unexpectantly.

"Seriously girl, I have fucking missed you! Where have you been? I can't believe it has been so long!" Adriana was always the loud one of the three of us, and clearly nothing had changed.

"Sorry hun, you know how it is…shit…time just flies, but honestly, I'm so happy that we worked this out." I said truthfully.

I had been in my own world lately and I had to admit that it felt good to reconnect with my friend. Out of the corner of my eye I noticed her boyfriend, Tristano. He was a Captain who flew private jets and was one of those guys who looked like he was straight out of a European fashion magazine.

Adriana was talking a mile a minute as she linked her arm through mine and led me towards the closest bar.

"Hi Tristano!" I called out over my shoulder. "Sorry, she's …" I motioned to Adri who was still talking, clearly not intending to waste a second. Tristano nodded and smiled as he collected my bags and followed us to the bar. When he caught up to us, he leaned over and kissed my cheek.

"Good to see you again, Samantha." He winked as he went in and got us a table.

"Adriana…." He drawled her name seductively as we all found seats. I watched as he stared at my friend with eyes that seemed to say so much more than words could. For a second, I felt like an outsider watching an intimate moment between lovers as they exchanged a knowing glance.

I silently wondered why all the guys I met were either total flakes or slimy assholes like Dave. They only seemed to ever want one thing and then be done with me. Why hadn't I found love like my friends had?

I hadn't always been so cynical. Early on in college I had been hopeful. Hopeful that I would find love, a love like my parents had. Even though they died when I was young, I clearly remembered how they would look at each other. It was with the same unspoken love that I now saw between Adri and Tristano. I thought that despite my awful experiences, maybe, just maybe, I could find that, too.

I didn't believe that anymore, though. After years of things not working out and always finding myself in the same space, I was frustrated, and truly thought that at this point I might be better off alone. *Besides,* began the voice at the back of my head, dripping with contempt, *your friends have so much more going for them than you do. They aren't carrying around the weight of a broken past.* I shook it off and buried it deep, as I always did, covering it all with a smile. I had to stay in the moment.

Keep your focus rock solid, Samantha. I whispered to the broken girl inside of me as I gave myself a mental kick in the ass.

"Okay, before we get into anything, I have to show you something!" Squealed Adri as she thrust her left hand in my face. A massive solitaire diamond adorned her ring finger and it sparkled just about as bright as her smile. Without waiting for me to even react, she continued.

"Can you believe it?" Adriana giggled. Tristano leaned in and slid a protective arm around my friend. The warmth that emanated from his eyes as he looked at her was both passion and love.

"Finally did it!" He added, his eyes sparkling with happiness and love.

"OMG, I am so happy for you guys!" I gushed. "When did this happen? Adri, I can't believe you didn't announce it! You literally post everything!" I teased her.

"Well, it was just two days ago and honestly, this is the first time we've left the house since it happened." She giggled.

I shook my head. Three years into their relationship and they were still in that nauseating phase. "And I guess your Wi-Fi was down?" I deadpanned.

Adri playfully punched my shoulder. "Don't be a bitch. We were just enjoying having this moment all to ourselves. And you should be honoured. Once I knew we were meeting up, I wanted you to be the first to know and see it in person."

"I am honored, babe." I whispered, the lump in my throat suddenly growing larger.

In the beginning, Adriana and Tristano had had difficulties getting their romance off the ground. There was so much drama between them that many people didn't know if it would last, but here they were, three years later and soaring above the clouds, happier than ever.

It dawned on me in that moment that I was the only one left of the three of us...

Ava had married Conor, Adri was now engaged to Tristano. And I hadn't even had a date in months. Not that I had wanted one. My life was about my work and I didn't have the time or the desire to date. Certainly not slimy creatures like Dave anyway.

"Seriously though, Sam." Adriana continued as if she was reading my mind. "Is there really no one in your life right now? What happened babe, you used to be out there as much as the next girl." She asked earnestly.

"Yeah, well, life took over I guess. I just haven't found anyone worth my time. Maybe Tristano has a friend for me..." I joked.

He looked at me with eyes that seemed to bore right through me. "Samantha..." He began. "There is someone very special out there for you, but you know, you'll never find him if you don't allow yourself to keep your eyes open."

From anyone else I would have been offended. However, I knew Tristano well enough to not take it personally. He had always been very direct and to the point. He was a man who didn't apologize or tiptoe around feelings. He was Alpha in every way. Men like that tended to both scare the shit out of me, and yet, were almost addictive in the aura they put out into the world. It was the same when I first met Conor, too. Yet, now that I knew both of these powerful men, I could see what my girlfriends loved about them.

HEATWAVE

They were the ultimate protectors and their love seemed to be a continuous wrap around the women they loved.

Sadly, I wasn't really sure what it was that I even wanted out of a relationship. I feared that I was too messed up to even have one.

The voice in my head always destroyed my chances anyway, making me remember the things I wanted to keep hidden, even from myself. Memories hit me in flashes, brief seconds of deep pain rising up to the surface, never visible to anyone but myself.

***

15 years ago…

He had been gentle and sweet at first, cuddling, tickling, making me giggle. I was too old at that point for such childish games, but I still loved the attention and the affection. That was one thing Gammy didn't provide…love. The essentials were taken care of, but I felt starved for love. When he noticed me, looked at me, winked at me like we shared a special secret, it felt good. I craved it and soaked up any attention he gave me. Even when that attention turned dark.

One night it was different. His hand slipped under the bottom of my shirt and rubbed up my back as he hugged me. Large fingers grazed the back of my training bra. I could still feel the shivers going up my spine, because I knew. Although I hadn't had a parent to guide me, I still knew what was right and what felt so terribly wrong. Yet, also good. It was as confusing as it was satisfying.

So, when his goodnight kiss went from my cheek to my lips, I let him linger. I smiled when he pulled back and brushed the hair from my face.

Gammy's disgust at my suggestions and disbelief at my accusations had been the beginning of the constant rumination of words in my head. First, she accused me of lying, but later, when he lost interest in me, her attitude and snarky remarks birthed "The Voice." *You know it's wrong and yet you let him. You're such a little whore, you liked it when he touched you, didn't you? You wanted it even more.*

I couldn't deny that she was right. His touch warmed parts of me that I didn't even know existed yet. And I let him. Until that day. The day he decided it was time. It had all happened so fast, the light touching, the eventual clandestine looks from across the table that held my school books we were supposed to be studying from.

I died that day.

I had just walked out of the bathroom, my period hitting me hard like it always did. And he was waiting for me. I remember smiling, thinking he would cuddle me and rub my belly as he had before, but I should have known he wouldn't remain satisfied with childish making out any longer.

"You're a woman now, Sammy." Even now, I winced, remembering the baby name he used for me. "You've had your period for months now. It's time…my sweet girl."

He had grabbed me and held me down with a pillow over my face, forceful and brutal. I cried and pleaded with him to stop. The sound of a zipper still made me tremble in fear. I had protested, claiming my period was already too painful, but that was what he wanted. He insisted it would make the cramps go away, and as I cried out in pain as he stretched my young body further than ever before, he had whispered in my ear.

"You'll think of me every time you bleed. For the rest of your life, you'll keep me inside you."

He was right.

***

My four-hour layover passed by in a flash, and soon it was time to get back on the plane and head out to Australia. I hugged my friend and her new fiancée hard.

"Promise that it won't be three years till we see each other in person again?" Adriana asked. "We haven't set a date for the wedding yet, but no matter when or where it is, you have to be there!"

"Agreed!" I smiled. I had to admit that a few hours with her had made me feel better than I had in months.

CASSIDY LONDON

Chapter 6

Australia

Ashton Chase

Two days later, Bradley asked me to meet him down at the station. Adrenaline coursed through my blood, filling me with that strange mix of excitement and nerves. I couldn't wait to get out there and start helping instead of just watching.

Bradley had been great up to now about not asking me too many questions, and although I had told him about my preference to keep my London life away from the interest of the station guys, I felt the need to reiterate it again. Not that I had much to hide, but I didn't appreciate people getting nosy and all up in my business. People tended to want to know it all. In my case, the more people knew about me, the more judgemental they got, and I wasn't interested in anyone's opinion. A quick text to Bradley just to remind him was enough.

You got it mate. He replied back. *You're just another regular joe from down at the pub.*

I smiled. I could hear him laughing through his text.

A hefty tip and an exchange of personal numbers ensured that Jack, the Uber guy from the airport, was waiting outside my house anytime I needed him. The less people I had to make small talk with the better.

Grabbing my bag, I locked the door and headed towards the car. With each step, I counted. Just like when I had entered for the first time, ten stairs from door to curb and twenty-seven steps total till the car. Shit like this was helpful when I needed to focus. Another reason that I didn't like to get too close to anyone. As soon as people started noticing my quirks, they quickly tried to change them. Especially women.

Which is why, to anyone watching, I hadn't had a girlfriend since Olivia. But of course, discretion in my sex life was one of my priorities. Back in London, I stuck to Sylvia's; a particular escort service that always had my back. Discreet and beautiful girls. No questions asked, willing to do anything I wanted and most importantly, they knew how to keep their mouths shut. I preferred it that way. Relationships were complicated because people were, or perhaps more specifically, I was. In any case, I'd have to take care of my own needs for a while. I wasn't familiar with the industry here and although Bradley was trustworthy, that was a new level of trust that I'd have to feel out and take my time with.

The station was only about thirty minutes from my place, which wasn't too bad. I thanked Jack and headed in to the station. Bradley saw me coming before I even had the chance to look for him.

"Ash!" He called. "Mate! Shit, I'm so glad to see you!" He grabbed me and pulled me into a bear hug. We fist bumped and hugged again. Damn, it was good to see my friend.

"How was the trip?" He asked. "You must be exhausted!"

"Not too bad. I've been able to recover. Your place is amazing. I slept a bit, got some work done. It was just enough time to get over the jet lag." I answered.

"Glad to hear it. I need to get you up to speed around here." He continued as he walked me through the station. "We've had a ton of volunteers coming in. Even boys on the job from Canada showed up earlier in the week."

"That's great, mate. Glad to hear it. Just tell me where I can be most helpful." I offered, truly willing to do anything required.

"Locals have been helping out where they can too, but honestly, my friend, I want to keep you on the front lines with me."

"You sure?" I asked. "You know that it's been years since I was out there fighting the flames. Not since we did it together in London." I reminded him.

"No worries, mate. Honestly, at this point, it's less technique and more the fact that we need more hands on-deck." He said truthfully.

I was taken aback but also honoured. He had said as much when we spoke on the phone, but now it was real. And for Bradley to have that kind of trust in me felt great. I couldn't let him down. I had to be on my game and ready for anything.

"Other than going into the hardest hit communities and helping them to evacuate, there's also the animals. I have a team that's going in and pulling out the ones that are still alive. You up for that too?" He continued as he made notes on his tablet.

"You know it. When I said I was here to help, it was in any capacity that was needed." I reiterated. And it was true. I would have said yes to anything that he needed. A sense of calm come over me. I was where I was supposed to be. So many other times in life I had felt pushed or obligated, but this was all me.
I could have stayed at home in the safety of my London flat, crunching numbers and trading inside a digital world. But something inside me wanted more. Wanted to help do something positive in this world that seemed to be crumbling. My world had crumbled too many times over. Some of it had been salvaged along the way, other parts had not. But maybe this was finally the time when I got to rebuild those parts that felt long lost.

Chapter 7

Australia

Samantha Jordan

The flight from San Francisco to Sydney was seventeen hours. I hadn't always been able to sleep on a plane, but this time was different. After weeks on night shift at the emergency hospital, I was a wreck and truly needed the time. As we touched down, the feel of the wheels on the ground made me smile. I was here. Back in the place that had once healed me, and now it was my time to give back. Finally, I would be able to help them heal.

I had received a message before boarding from the NSW Sydney Animal Clinic. It included a complete list of what I should expect and how the hospital had been operating to date. I spent part of the flight reviewing the documents and learning about the methods they had put in place. Obviously, there wasn't enough room in the ER, or any vet clinic really, for the number of animals that were arriving so they had to make do. Volunteers had brought in laundry baskets for the recovering koalas and local DIYers had helped to build outdoor enclosures for the animals to recover in. Blankets and many other basic supplies were still needed daily. Thankfully, the world had responded, and every day new packages were arriving on the doorstep of the clinic.

Their numbers were always fluctuating. More animals came in and others didn't make it out. Overall, they were looking at saving thousands, yet it still wasn't enough. Billions had already been wiped out. Just saying the words in my head sent my emotions spiralling out of whack. I knew I had to keep a clear head in order to do my best, but at the same time, I had a strong feeling that I would be crying into my pillow each night. At least there wouldn't be any distractions here. The people I'd be working with were all on the same page, all about the animals. There would be no Dave's to follow me around, lurking in the halls, making me nervous. I could leave all that behind me and focus on the job that I was here to do.

As soon as I had made it through customs I headed outside. The heat hit me like a ton of bricks and I instantly felt sick to my stomach. It was nauseating, and I could only imagine how much hotter it was out on the front lines. After hailing a cab and loading it up with my luggage, I asked the cabbie to take me straight to the clinic. As my cab drove along, I watched outside as the sky went from grey to black and even to red in some places. It was truly horrifying and somewhat apocalyptic.

All the media pictures had been accurate. A part of me had hoped that things were being blown out of proportion the way they always say that media is fabricating shit…well, I had hoped this was that same shit. No such luck. This was bad. In some areas, it literally looked like recovery would be impossible. A part of me felt fear creeping up the back of my neck as I silently wondered if I had made the right decision.

Finally, we pulled up in front of the clinic. This was it. Everything I'd been waiting for was finally in place. No more messing around and wishing to be here, the time was now and I was ready. I took a deep breath, paid the cab driver, grabbed my luggage, and marched right in, my head high, ready to dive in.

I don't know what I expected when I opened those doors. After all, I worked in the ER at home, this scene shouldn't have been all that different. But it was.

This was nothing like home. No large interior welcoming lobby, no sense of calm and order. I had walked into Hades and none of those rules applied. Instead of dogs and cats in the waiting area, there was wildlife. *Everywhere.* The large expanse of a lobby had been transformed into a makeshift triage center complete with enclosures that held sad little koalas gripping blankets and a few leaves. My heart lurched out of my ribcage as I saw them. Making eye contact with those beautiful little faces and instantly feeling their stress and pain was not what I had expected upon walking through the front door.

I stood frozen for a few minutes until I heard a woman's voice in the far-off distance.

"Excuse me? Miss? Miss?" She continued moving closer towards me.

"This is not an open vet hospital anymore. You'll have to go elsewhere. We are closed to the public." She continued as she linked her arm in mine and began trying to walk me out.

Shaking my head to stop her, I finally found my voice. "No, you don't understand, I'm here to help. I'm a doctor from the US. I spoke with someone...."

Shit! What the hell was his name? Steve? I could remember the name of all the fur baby patients and their issues, but god help me to remember a random human's name. I began fumbling through my purse to find my phone. A few quick email scrolls and I showed her the confirmation that I had received back home.

Dr. Joel Watson. How could I forget? I chastised myself for being so stupid.

"Oh my goodness, I'm so sorry! I had no idea we were expecting help today! You came from America? Alone? Really?" She seemed excited and was babbling away as she led me through the building.

"Well, yes..." I smiled.

Alone? I thought. *Did she expect a group?*

"When did you arrive?" She continued, moving towards the elevators.

"Actually, just a couple of hours ago. I jumped in a cab and came right here." I finished as I stifled a yawn which seemed oddly out of place as I had pretty much slept the whole way.

"I had been wanting to come and help somehow. Australia is one of my favorite places. I actually did an internship here in my last year of school." I continued, now babbling along as much as her. "I had reached out to my contacts, but no one had answered. I wasn't sure what to do next when I received this application notice at my clinic."

We approached an office and she ushered me in. "Just wait here, love, someone will be with you in just a moment."

As I sat alone in the office and waited, I couldn't help but smile wide, so much so that my cheeks hurt. I wanted to get started right away. Those little koalas that I had seen were just the tip of the iceberg that we had to save, and I knew there wasn't any time to waste.

But like anything, paperwork takes time. So, by the time I had spoken to all the right people, and they had verified my claims, read my documents and certifications, and signed me on, it was two hours later.

Fortunately, there was an apartment building just down the street from the hospital that was typically a housing refuge for those on overnight call shifts. I was introduced to Allison, the vet who had been matched with me. She walked me over, making small talk along the way.

"So, you're from America, huh? I just arrived, too. I'm from the Northern Territories, would love to get to America one day." I nodded, straining to try and understand her accent. She seemed pleasant, but her accent was so strong that I felt like I was missing every second word.

We were in apartment 2B. She said that the last person to stay there was a vet tech whose family ended up being evacuated back in Queensland. She had left in a hurry to go and help her family, leaving Allison alone and a space available. Fortunately, it was a two bedroom so I would have my own space to retreat to.

It was a pretty basic apartment. Furnished, but barely. But it didn't matter, all I needed was a safe, clean place to rest my head at night. Other than that, I was here to work and I couldn't wait to get started.

Chapter 8

Australia

Ashton Chase

When I arrived at the station, I was dressed only in cargo shorts and a white t-shirt, but all my essentials were in my overnight bag. I'd be staying at the firehouse for the next week, so I had extra clothes, toiletries, and my laptop. Aside from that, there wasn't too much that I needed to bring with me.

As promised, Bradley gave me my own room. Typically, firefighters had to share space, but they did have a single room that Bradley had been using. He graciously offered to switch with me so I could have some personal space. He had no idea how grateful I was. The less social interaction the better.

After a quick chat, we did the rounds and Bradley introduced me to the guys. I was simply Ash from London, an old friend of his that he worked with back in the day. Nothing more or less. The troop seemed like a bunch of solid guys and I found myself actually looking forward to working alongside them. We spent a couple of hours helping me get reacquainted with the truck, how to use everything, and their methods. Most things worked the same as I remembered but with better technology than we had years ago.

Over lunch, the guys talked mostly about women. Some were married or in relationships but many others were young, single, and eager to show off. I kept to myself and didn't add much to the conversation. Until someone asked, of course.

"Well," I began, "honestly, I'm not a relationship kind of guy. I prefer to get my needs tended to and be on my way if you know what I mean." I said vaguely, swigging back my Coke.

"Yeah, we all say that until we meet the right girl." said Daniel, one of the guys who apparently had been with his high school sweetheart since they were in diapers.

"Like you did back in preschool, Dan?" Someone else chided him.

"Fuck you man." Dan responded. "At least I have a woman who loves me and is eager to see me at the end of the day. What do you have?" He challenged them.

"A fucking dog, mate! I have a fucking dog!" Answered a guy named Rob from the back of the room as everyone exploded into laughter.

Bradley slapped me on the back as he got up to serve himself more lunch. "So happy you're here, my friend. I really am."

We had to wait until the team that was in the field was due back, then we would be heading out to replace them. Finally, it was time. We packed up the truck, loaded up our gear, and climbed in. It seemed crazy that just a short distance away we would find hell on earth. The sky became redder the closer we got and the air filled with billowing clouds of black smoke. The heat began to feel scorching even in the shade. The visceral feeling of being so close to fire is something that you never forget.

My mind began to waver in its control, so I did what I knew best and began to silently count the strings of thread that were visible along the bottom of my jacket.

1...2...3... by the time I had hit the hundreds, we were there. Our destination. I was ready. No more time to think, survival and retrieval the only things running my brain. We jumped from the truck, pulled out the hose, and began our work. As some of the guys focused on water, my smaller team was on retrieval. We headed out into the scorched forest to look and listen for lives who needed us. And not five minutes in, I heard him. His cries were like that of a newborn babe. He was clinging to a branch about halfway up.

I silently thanked my personal trainer back in London for insisting that I install a vertical rope climb in my home gym. At first, I thought he was crazy. Then he convinced me and the first time I tried, I fell flat on my face. But after months of training, I was like a monkey in a tree. My first day on the scene in Australia was no exception.

"Forget that one, man, get the others that are lower down." Said one of the guys running by. Other trees had lower branches, making it easier to climb up. "You'll never make it to that one. Besides... look." He pointed up. Behind a mass of singed wood was a large paw with long nails poking out.

"It's the mother, dude. Looks like she didn't make it."

The mother koala was hanging lifeless in the tree. Her fur was mostly gone and the burns on her body showed a clear sign that she never had a chance. But somehow, this tiny little one peeking out was alive and calling for help. He was so small it was hard to see what his injuries could even be. If this little guy had survived, it was because he was protected by his mother's body. There was no way I was leaving him there. Mama koala had done her job flawlessly till the end and I wouldn't be the one to fail her now. Emotion spread through me as I fought back tears. This was what a mother was supposed to do. Not save herself and leave her flesh and blood behind.

I said a silent prayer for mama koala's soul and took a few steps back in preparation.

"What you doing, mate?" called out the guys.

"You don't think you're going to run up a damn tree, do ya'?" Another called out.

"He knows they are unstable after the fire, right?" I heard someone ask Bradley. "It's like firefighting 101!" The cocky jerk called out.

"Mind your own business." I spat back. "I don't have much to lose and I came here to do a job. I'm not prepared to leave that little guy to die."

I backed up just enough to give myself solid momentum and I went for it. A running leap on to the trunk, my hands wrapping around it as I inched my hips and hiked my legs up one then the other until I was almost at the first branch. I hung on with my strength as I reached out a hand to the little guy.

"Come on buddy, you can do it." I cooed to him. "Your mama wanted you to live, you got this. Come on buddy, just a little more…" I coaxed him as he inched closer.

The second I could feel his little paw in my hand, I gently tugged, and he dropped easily onto my shoulder. Within seconds, he had climbed around my back and was gripping my jacket with his small nails. Still squeaking, he nuzzled his face into the back of my neck and I felt him exhale. Slowly and gently, I let myself slide down the tree trunk. Fortunately, this was a tree where only half of it was burnt. The fire must have turned at the last second. A few seconds more and the mother's efforts would have been all for nothing.

As soon as I was back on the ground, everyone crowded around to see the little guy. He was clearly in need of medical help for smoke inhalation at the very least, not to mention that a baby this small needed his mother's milk. I was going to have to move quickly.

"Hey Bradley!" Someone called out. "Your mate here is a regular Steve Irwin!"

I smiled. Little did these guys know how much it meant to me to save a little one's life. Paying it forward had been my life's mission when I was on the force in London, and I was thrilled to be able to do it again.

I didn't have too long to revel in the moment, though. One of the other trucks was leaving for the animal hospital and I needed to get Lucky, as I was already calling him in my mind, onboard. We typically put the survivors in cages for the drive, but this was a different situation.

"As much as I need you here, bro, I know this little guy needs extra special help." Began Bradley. We both knew that we couldn't just put him in a cage, he was too small and weak. Clinging to me like he would his mother, his eyes were wide with fear and pain. He had a long road ahead of him and the first step was to get him to emergency in one piece. I would have to go with him.

Chapter 9

Australia

Samantha Jordan

It had already been three weeks since I touched down on Australian soil and the time had just flown by. Long hours at the urgent care center made each day bleed into the next without reprieve. Sometimes I went back to my apartment to rest, other times I slept at the clinic. We didn't have a nice locker room with privacy like back home. Here it was literally just a single cot in the back of an unused office filled with paperwork a mile high that needed filing. Occasionally, I had a few hours or an evening with Allison. We typically ordered Asian food and drank wine until we fell asleep on the couch, most of the time still in our scrubs.

The day everything changed was nothing I could have anticipated. There had been many unexpected events in my life and most, if not all of them, had been awful. But this one came out of nowhere, hit me square in the face, and left me a quivering mess of *feeling*.

I had been standing outside the main gate waiting for the latest truck to come in with more rescued animals. They had called ahead and told us they had a group of a dozen or so in the truck and all in various stages of distress. There was everything from first to third degree burns, orphans crying for their moms, and a certain number that were most likely not going to make it. Those were the ones that got to me the most.

Their sad little eyes begging for relief. Euthanizing an animal that is begging for help was the most heartbreaking thing, but sometimes it was necessary. And in the case of the Australian apocalypse, it was far more common than we initially expected.

But what wasn't expected was the very first man who got out of the truck. Typically, these trucks were driven by wildlife rescuers, yet the first guy I saw was a fireman. Actually, in those first few moments, I couldn't have told you what or who it was that I saw. I just *FELT*.

He stood there looking down at the blanketed figure in his arms. A lock of dark, messy hair fell across the front of his tanned, chiseled face. His skin was covered in smoky dirt but when his gaze lifted, the bluest eyes I'd ever seen came peering out in my direction. We locked eyes and he held me there, his presence overwhelming my senses. Like the pages of the Australian firefighter calendar come to life, I felt transported into a living, breathing fantasy. A white tank top covered in smoky ash accentuated biceps of steel, and his stance, while confident and imposing, starkly contrasted the softness with which he cradled the tiny blanketed form. My skin prickled and I felt chilled despite the heated Australian sun. My lungs suddenly constricted, making each breath painful. Handsome didn't cut it. This man was a god.

My reaction to him both enthralled and confused me. A lump formed at the back of my throat, making it hard to swallow. Something was off, way off. This wasn't me. I didn't get flustered over men.

Other women in their twenties were all about getting a man, keeping one, marrying one, and having babies. Or, they were on the opposite end of the spectrum, looking to hook up left right and center, one-night stands, and game playing. Neither side interested me.

Granted, during my early college days and for a while after, I had tried to be like them. But it was a farce, a front. Reality was that men just didn't get me. I was always on guard, worried about what I said, did, what they wanted. And then there was the fear. Fear of guys like Dave. Those were slimy bastards that I was forever terrified of encountering. I knew it tripped me up and pushed away a lot of good guys, but often it felt out of my control.

Regardless, none to date had ever made me feel like I did in that moment. Like I was melting the second he entered my field of vision. Maybe it was the Australian sun or the nearby bushfire heat. *Maybe…* I lied to myself. But honestly, every part of my soul knew better.

The other men in the truck had started emptying out baskets of koalas', wombats, and little joeys. Many were crying in pain. We needed to move fast or we would lose more of these little guys than we could save. I had to snap out of it and move quickly. I attempted to shake off the spell of this Adonis-like man as I ran over to the guys unloading the truck. Someone handed me a large crate with a mom and baby kangaroo inside. Upon a quick glance, I could see that moms' paws were totally burned, the pads under her feet hanging on by a thread. Her baby was still in his pouch, barely peeking out. Both had singed fur and smelled like a combination of ash and burnt flesh.

After dropping the first basket off in triage, I headed back out to the truck. He was still there, holding that blanket close to his chest and staring…*at me*. This time, I couldn't shake it off. On Jell-O legs I moved forward, each step as painful as it was captivating. Those sparkling blue eyes stayed locked on mine, silently pulling me forward. I felt like I was falling into deep ocean pools and it was mesmerizing.

There was a moment where time seemed to stand still as we both just stood there, falling into each other's eyes. I could have stayed there forever.

Chapter 10

Australia

Ashton Chase

She was an angel. A fucking angel with a goddam aura of sin surrounding her. All of a sudden, my heart beat so loudly, I was afraid she would hear it. And when she raised her eyes and locked on to mine... I knew right there that she would be the woman who would forever change my world. Chestnut brown waves brought together in a simple ponytail that I wanted to wrap my fingers around. A slender but athletic body and curves that screamed to be touched. My mind flashed with images of naked skin as my mouth watered to know the sweetness of her flavour. But it was the warmth and sincerity in her eyes that felt like...*home*. And all I wanted to do was wrap my arms around her and never let her go. This strange mix of uncontrollable lust and a deep need to protect was new to me. It left me nervous and unstable.

Who was this perfect creature staring back at me? I had to know.

And why was I having such a hard time breathing? Women typically didn't affect me like this. Not that I hadn't felt deep attraction. Although I wasn't a life of the party type of guy, I knew what I liked. The two girls that I always asked for back in London were similar in their look. Dirty blond, curvy, and not too chatty. But now, everything I had ever liked was suddenly inconsequential.

This girl in front of me definitely didn't fit the description of my typical type, but something about her made my heart beat faster and my body stir. She was petite in height compared to the leggy blondes that I usually favoured. She was simple and straightforward in her scrubs. Her face was void of any visible makeup, yet her beauty radiated with an energy that I could feel. Round, perky breasts raised and lowered as I watched her breathe. She looked young but just enough. Staring at her made me forget why I was there. She seemed to be frozen too, but only for a moment. Then she moved off to help the other guys, giving me a minute or two to regain my composure. And I thought I had, until she spoke.

"What do you have in there?" She asked, motioning to the blanket. Her American accent took me off guard for yet another second.

"Oh shit. Sorry, yeah right, so it's an orphaned koala, not sure how young but we found it alone in a tree crying out." I stumbled over my words and silently cursed myself for sounding like an idiot.

"Did you catch sight of the mother at all?" She inquired, edging closer to look inside the makeshift carrier.

I could smell the fresh flowery scent of shampoo and body lotion as she moved closer. I inhaled deeply, only realizing my mistake when my cock hardened at her scent.

I cleared my throat. "Yeah, she'd been completely burned, but this little guy survived by being trapped beneath her scorched body. It was like she died trying to protect him."

HEATWAVE

My voice trailed off a bit. I hesitated again. *Damn, this woman was making me nervous!*

She had a sweet, honest demeanour that I hadn't seen in a long time, or maybe even ever…I wanted to know more. She was clearly American by her accent, yet living and working here. Was she an ex-pat? Or like myself, visiting help from abroad? Did she have a boyfriend? Questions flew through my mind as I tried to sort them into which would be appropriate and which would have to wait. But there was no time to be selfish.

"Tell me more about where you found him." She said, removing the tightly wound blanketed baby from my arms. His little head peeked out, tiny little eyes that searched from right to left, before his tiny cry pierced the air.

I cleared my throat. "I named him Lucky… because he was." I began before going through the story. What I didn't tell her, of course, was that I had insisted on saving him because I understood the expression on his little face was more than just the physical pain. As I spoke, emotions from my past began to mix with the heat of the moment, and I could feel my control slipping. I needed to leave. But not without knowing her name. Clearing my throat, I did what I hadn't done in years, "I didn't get your name?" I asked as casually as I could.

"Um…" She hesitated. I knew what that meant, she didn't want to give it. *Smart girl.* I liked her even more.

"Yeah, so I'm the doctor on call tonight. Dr. Jordan. Samantha Jordan." She stumbled a little, smiled, and for just a second, didn't quite seem like the put together, confident doctor who had initially walked out of the building when I showed up.

The baby koala had now moved from my arms to hers, but not much else had changed. He was still squealing and we were still caught in the stare down like two wild animals in the headlights.

What was happening here? There was only one answer. I would definitely be seeing Dr. Samantha Jordan again, and preferably without her scrubs on.

Chapter 11

Australia

Samantha Jordan

I think I might have run back into the clinic. In fact, I'm sure that I did. I was only semi-aware that had I mumbled something about having to get the little koala inside before I turned and bolted. If I had stood there any longer, I might have melted into the ground, and it definitely wouldn't have been from the heat of the Australian bushfire.

My heart was racing, sweat was forming in all the places it shouldn't, and there was a throbbing in all the most intimate areas of my body. But that was nothing compared to the level of crazy in my mind. It felt like hundreds of questions and hypothetical answers were weaving in and out of my consciousness.

Who was that guy and what had he done to me?

But I had a job to do and this little guy and all his friends needed me at my best. Thankfully, working helped. It kept me busy for a solid hour and the work helped to quell the chaos of my mind. The older koalas that had come in with him were severely burnt and in need of immediate attention, and in some cases, surgery.

After it was all said and done, I checked in on little Lucky again. He was still whimpering, but now it was mostly a call for his mama. My heart broke for his newfound situation and the long road of life he was now staring down. Any injured animal had my heart, but this little guy seemed special, and I made it my mission to see to it myself that he would be okay. I spent time holding and cuddling him after his physical, and feeding him a bottle of milk, which thankfully we had several of on hand. Then I wrapped him up in a makeshift pouch and placed him in a laundry basket. It was a small enclosure with leaves placed around him to make him feel more at home. Lucky was already sleeping and I hoped it would be a long nap. Closing the door gingerly, I headed back down the hall and into the ER, my mind never far from both Lucky and his fireman saviour.

Typical me would have moved on to work without another thought, but something about this guy kept me stuck on him. And it wasn't just his good looks. Sure, he was hot, but it was something more. His imposing presence perhaps? The way he took up space without saying a word? Or maybe the fact that he had asked for my name but I didn't have the whereabouts to ask for his. Who was this guy? He had been traveling with the wildlife conservationists. Typically, firemen weren't the ones showing up with injured animals. In the weeks since I'd arrived, I hadn't seen one do that before. Would he be back?

For Christ's sake, Sam, get your shit together. This is a warzone and you're stuck on some guy? So not like you and so the wrong time! Began my brain. Once it started, it didn't rain, it poured. The voice appeared and brought with her many new weapons, cackling with glee.

HEATWAVE

You're not stuck on a guy, Samantha Jordan, you're looking for a pity fuck, aren't you? Always spreading your legs the first chance you get. When will you realize that they won't like you anyway?

Her biting words made me wince in what felt like actual, physical pain.

I shook it off for the second time that day. But hours had passed and I was no closer to forgetting him. As I worked diligently on a large male koala, spreading cream on his burns and bandaging his feet, I repeated to myself that I was here to do a job and nothing more.

***

One day seemed to bleed into the next at the clinic. Some days there were more surgeries, other days it was constant bandaging. As much as I kept up my positive attitude in public, there were times inside when I was in absolute terror. It was a never-ending stream of wildlife, to the point that we all began wonder if there were going to be any left at all. We were starting to hit full capacity, and now had to transfer out the animals that were healing. If we didn't, we would find ourselves unable to continue our work.

It was at a lunch meeting between the doctors that we got the news we'd been waiting for.
Dr. Ben Bottsmann, one of the senior vets on staff, delivered the good news. And being that it was our first really good news in weeks, it lifted everyone's spirits as much as it did mine.

"Well ladies and gents, it looks like we have hit the magic number! We have officially treated five thousand animals. Not all have lived, of course, which is the sad reality of a job like this. However, we have done our best and I am proud of the work we have done here. The Australia Zoo has contacted us, and they'll be sending down trucks to pick up the animals who are ready to be moved on to proper rehabilitation. As we all know, the Australia Zoo has one of the best sanctuaries in the country and I couldn't be prouder to send off these little guys to them. They will have a good home there and hopefully, when the time is right, some may even end up back in the wild where they belong." He paused as the room exploded with applause.

"You have all been an integral part of saving them, and I hope that's something you carry through in all your work from here on. You have made a difference, because making a difference is often not on a grand scale but to a single individual. And those of you who have come from across the world to help us…" He paused as he looked at myself and the four other doctors who had done the same.

"Your efforts and commitment have not gone unnoticed. We appreciate you and know that if you needed the same, I believe many people in this room would come to your aid, too."

Dr. Ben's words struck a chord so deep that I had to fight to stay professional. Emotion welled up inside me as I fought to smile, nod, and push it back down. I had made a difference and it was worth it. It was pretty much everything I needed to hear.

Chapter 12

Australia

Ashton Chase

Dr. Samantha Jordan. Her name was on repeat in my head the entire drive through the backcountry. Visons of her danced in my head. That simple yet fragrant aroma that had enveloped my senses now seemed engrained in my head despite the stench of ash and death that surrounded me. The way she held Lucky, the baby koala, so gingerly and pressed her nose to his as she cooed sounds of love at him. It was eating me up, and the uncertainty and surprise of my reaction wasn't helping the case.

We made it back in record time and worked for another six hours. Finally, after more search and rescue than I could have imagined was ever needed, we boarded the truck and headed back to the station. The days that followed were pretty much the same. I stayed at the station until the end of the week before gaining a few days off to rest up at home.

While on duty, we had found more animals and sent them off to various clinics, but I hadn't been back to the NSW Sydney Animal Clinic since that very first day. Not for lack of wanting, but only because we were now in the small towns, helping families to evacuate.

It was good because it had given me time to think. That's what I needed, time to absorb my feelings and plan my next move. Life was like a game of chess and I liked to think through my moves before I made my play.

Now that I had some time off coming to me, I was eager to get back to Bondi Beach and Bradley's condo. Not just to recharge, but I needed to spend time working with my London team. I had been doing quick daily check ins with them from the privacy of my room at the station, but I needed more. I needed face to face personal calls. My clients needed to know I was there for them. But also, 24/7 was taking a toll on me. I needed to rest, workout, and make sure I was at my best in all areas. I wasn't going to fail. Not at my job or as a firefighter or with the beautiful Dr. Jordan.

But I needed a plan, a reason to go back there, and a way to make it perfect. My mind was going a mile a minute trying to plan it out. But as fast as that was happening, I was also skeptical. Why did I want to go back there? Was it more than just the physical? I hadn't had a relationship since Olivia and I certainly didn't want to start now, especially as this was a temporary situation for me. I wasn't going to stay in Australia longer than I had to. Help with the crisis and get out, that had always been the plan. But all of a sudden, I was facing a situation that I wasn't sure I could handle. If I went back there, she would probably ask questions, and I definitely wasn't prepared to offer any answers.

***

Back at the condo, I dropped my gear and set out for a run on the beach. I needed to get my head screwed on right. This woman was like a siren, calling to me in ways I had never heard before. My body was wrecked and my mind on edge. Running was the only answer. I started out slow but soon picked up speed despite the heat.

Working on Bradley's team over the past week had been hard training. Carrying the hoses, lifting the kangaroos, and moving rubble had been brutal on the body. But it made for an easier run.

I picked up speed as I headed on to the boardwalk. *Dr. Samantha Jordan.* Her name was on repeat in my head. I knew in my soul that I couldn't deny the feelings I was having. Not even Olivia had produced such a visceral reaction in me. I knew it was crazy, but here I was, completely overwhelmed by a woman I had met for just a few minutes. Was it just her unparalleled beauty? Or was it more? I had to know.

And that's how I made my decision. I would go back there and ask her to join me for dinner. When the questions came up, I would tell her the same things the guys at the station knew about me. There was no sense in telling the truth. I didn't need a woman getting all excited about a future with a wealthy man over a dinner. I had learned long ago that divulging too much too soon only resulted in disappointment and pain. But despite that, I would get what I wanted. And that was Samantha Jordan.

Chapter 13

Australia

Samantha Jordan

Days passed and if I was being honest, I looked for him. I had hoped and even wished that he would show up with more animals. The practical part of me knew it was useless, though. Firemen were out there on the front lines, saving lives, not running back to vet hospitals to talk to flustered doctors. Still, I hoped. And every day I checked on Lucky. He was actually doing quite well. After being treated for smoke inhalation and being fed regularly, he was actually thriving, a little lonely but thriving nonetheless. I made a point to get into his enclosure with him and cuddle him whenever I could. Usually early morning shifts and late at night before leaving. Basically, whenever I had a minute or two to myself, I'd spend it with Lucky.

And then about a week later, just as I was starting to forget, well, not really forget but purposefully forget, I got a call.

"Paging Dr. Jordan. Dr. Samantha Jordan to emergency, please!" came the voice over the loudspeaker.

I had been in the cafeteria when my name was called. The damn thing was so loud that I dropped my sandwich and nearly choked on my own spit. I had always been easily flustered and the PA system around here didn't help my case.

I quickly shot the rest of my soggy sandwich into the trash and began jogging down the hall. A call like that was never a good thing. Maybe a problem in triage, a need for an extra pair of hands, or even someone with an unruly dog, but a vet's life was anything but predictable.

The only thing that I was unprepared for was *HIM*.

Standing in the front entrance, wearing a white polo shirt and dark navy cargo shorts that were slung low on his hips, he took up space like no one else could. His shirt clung to his chest in all the right places, making my mouth go dry in an instant. With his aviators on, he looked like a runway model or maybe a handsome doctor in a tv show. With his hands pushed deep into his pockets, he paced up and down in front of the registration counter.

For a minute I was frozen in place. My legs felt like lead even though my heart began to beat right out of my chest and my mind screamed at me to run to him. This was insane. He still hadn't seen me, so I took a deep breath and drank him in. A tanned muscular leg came out from behind the counter as he paced, a classy looking boat shoe on the end. He moved with grace and agility and a confidence that didn't seem to fit the image he had left in my mind the first time I saw him. Gone was the sexy, rugged firefighter and in his place was a gorgeous gentleman that seemed to have stepped off the pages of a lifestyle magazine. Both versions made my mouth water and I wasn't sure which I wanted more.

As I stood there, chewing on my lip and trying to decide what I would say, he looked in my direction. All thoughts ceased to exist and once again I felt myself falling into a black hole. His presence left a visceral scar and the smirk that slowly spread across his face suggested that he knew it.

I quickly smoothed out the wrinkles in my scrubs, desperately wishing there was a way to freshen up, but no such luck. He'd seen me and was now marching forward in my direction. I willed my legs to move but nothing. I silently wondered what my breath was like. After coming off a double shift, I knew I looked like shit and chances were that no stick of gum could have been able to help me.

"Hey!" I heard myself call out as he approached. *Fuck.* I knew I sounded as eager as a goddam golden retriever. *Why had I said that?*

But instead of laughing, he smiled and slowly slid his glasses down that perfect bone structure. His smile widened and his eyes twinkled with confidence as he approached. He stopped slightly too close and stood still, forcing me to crane my neck to look up at him.

"Hello, Dr. Jordan." His deep voice resonated off the walls, leaving a constant vibration throughout my body. Hearing my name roll off his lips was by far the sexiest sound I'd heard all day, all week, possibly ever. With nothing more than my name, this man had awakened something inside me that I truly thought had never been there in the first place.

Forcing myself to focus, I answered. "Hi there." *Shit.* I didn't even know his name!

"Samantha."

His accent made me do a double take. How had I not noticed it the first time? He sounded different. Not Australian, definitely not American. British maybe? I wasn't sure.

I tried to respond, but all I could muster was a stutter and I felt myself flush with heat.

Then he did something unexpected. He pointed at me then tapped his lips and winked. It was like a secret code and fuck me, of course I didn't have the password.

"I'm sorry? What? Wha?" I stumbled again, unsure of what he was trying to tell me.

"Right here…you have something…may I?" He asked, although I wasn't sure what he was referring to. But I didn't need to wait long to figure it out. His hand reached up and with the pad of his thumb, he grazed my bottom lip. Fire lit up my insides, my chest heaved, and I could have sworn that my nipples hardened. I thought I would self-combust, but instead I made a sickening, breathless sound and jumped in the air like a frightened cat.

"My apologies for touching you. I didn't mean to scare you." He said as he quickly retracted his hand and stepped back.

Embarrassment washed over me and I stood there like such a fool. I wanted to run but my legs held fast to the ground through some invisible, magnetic force field.

"What time do you finish work today?" He asked before I could even catch my breath.

"Uhm… later tonight." I somehow mumbled softly.

"Good. I want to take you to dinner. Tonight."

He barely gave me a chance to answer before continuing on. "I'll check the time with the front desk and be here to pick you up."

Then just like that, he turned and walked out. The automatic doors slammed shut behind him before I even had the chance to truly comprehend what was happening.

CASSIDY LONDON

Chapter 14

Australia

Ashton Chase

Well, I had gotten what I wanted, but fuck if I hadn't left out some major details in the process. As I walked away, I realized that I hadn't given her my name or planned out where to take her. Something about this woman was seriously inhibiting my ability to think straight. Stopping to look up at the sky, I ran my fingers through my hair and tried to shake the cobwebs from my brain. I felt muted around her, like her light was too bright for me.

Pulling my phone from my back pocket, I dialed Bradley's number. Chances of him picking up right away were slim since I knew he was on a rest day, too. Fortunately, he picked up right away.

"Ash! Good to hear from you! I was planning to call you later." He answered, all chipper and happy.

"Really? Oh…okay then." I stumbled a little, taken off guard.

"Yeah, some of the guys and I are headed down to our favorite pub later. It's actually rather close to Bondi. Will you join us?"

"Thanks mate. That's really generous of you but actually, I already have plans. Well, sort of…it's why I was calling you, actually." I volunteered vaguely.

"Plans?" Bradley's voice practically raised an octave. "Shit, you old dog! I knew it! I knew you'd manage to find a girl. Who is she? How and where did you find her? Christ! You've been with me and the guys since you arrived. How'd you find the time? Not to mention, when was the last time you took a girl out?"

Bradley just kept running his mouth. I sighed, silently holding it together as he ranted. Moments like these were why I preferred to keep my private life separate. But I needed his recommendations.

"Yeah, I suppose it's uncommon to drop off an injured animal and meet a beautiful woman at the local vet clinic." I chuckled, trying to seem casual.

"Even more so in the middle of a fucking national climate apocalypse!" Bradley agreed.

I couldn't deny that.

"So anyway, I need restaurant recommendations for tonight. I just confirmed that I'm picking her up later this evening. But where should I take her? I want something with a great view but not casual, something classy."

"Iceberg's, mate! It's a great spot, it overlooks the ocean, upscale, great food; they have it all."

"Perfect. Thanks, Bradley." I was about to hang up when he called out to me.

"Hang on, Ash!"

"Sorry, what's that?" I asked, holding the phone back up to my ear.

"The team that took over from ours is having some trouble. Paul called me from the station earlier. He asked if I could come back early with a couple of guys."

Bradley paused. I knew what he was trying to ask.

"Of course, my friend. You can count on me. I'll do it." I offered immediately. After all, this was my whole reason for coming to Australia.

"Great, thanks mate. I'll need you there midday tomorrow. Apologies if that cuts your date short." He jested.

I laughed, "That's not what this is about, but thanks. See you tomorrow, Bradley." When I closed the phone, I felt uneasy. *Why had I said that?*

Samantha Jordan certainly made me want to rip her clothes off every time I looked at her. But she also ignited parts of me that had been dormant for a long time. Something was brewing in my heart with this girl and it was confusing the hell out of me.

Why was I doing this? I could have called a local escort service to have my needs tended to, just like I always had in London. *Because this is more than sex, Ashton.* Fuck it. I pushed those thoughts to the back of my mind. That's not how this would go down. I still needed to take it slow and keep my identity a secret. This had to be nothing more than a travel hook-up.

Chapter 15

Australia

Samantha Jordan

To say he had left me flustered for the rest of my shift would have been an understatement. I thought about him all afternoon. Every time someone called my name, I imagined it was him. Every time I walked down a hallway, my mind imagined that he was walking towards me. I inhaled and instead of the smell of antiseptic, that fresh mix of manliness and cleanliness somehow invaded my senses.

I just wished that I had told him to give me some time after my shift ended. There was a three-hour surgery booked at the end of my day and I knew I'd need to shower and change before going out. But now I was stuck. And I still didn't know this guy's name! What the hell? I didn't know his name, or have his number, or any goddam information about him. And as much as that frustrated the practical side of me, I was still floating on air like a school girl in love. Something about this man was really messing with my ability to think straight. I could even feel him invading my body. My breasts ached and my nipples tingled every time he crossed my mind. Not to mention the heat that was building up between my legs was almost unbearable. Sitting across from him at dinner was going to be unbearable.

I sighed. *Beautifully, perfectly, unbearable.*

***

The hours passed and before long, surgery was finishing up. The little kangaroo that we had been working on was going to wake up minus one front paw. Poor guy. It would be quite the shock but at least he would recover to hop around again.

I cleaned up, grabbed my purse from my locker, and made my way to the front entrance. It was only 6:30pm. I had decided that I'd tell him I was going home and he'd have to wait. He hadn't given me much of choice earlier so it was only fair that I did the same to him. There was no way I'd be going out without a shower and change of clothes.

As I made my way to the front, it was his damn smell that hit me first. I sucked in air, trying to steady myself, but it was no use. His presence affected me in ways I wasn't used to.

Standing in the doorway again, filling it up with both his physicality and his confidence, he was attracting a lot of attention. All the women, from the receptionists to the nurses and doctors as well as probably any woman in a five-mile radius, were giggling to each other.

He had changed from his polo shirt and shorts to navy blue dress pants and a button-down shirt. It was a crisp white and had the marks of an iron across the sleeve. What kind of firefighter had time to iron his shirts during a time like this? I wondered.

He smiled. "Samantha." The way he said my name sent shivers down my spine. I exhaled slowly, trying to remain focused.

"Hi…I'm sorry…" I stammered. "I don't even know your name…" It hadn't come out as smoothly as I had hoped. Oh well.

"That's because I didn't tell you my name."

His response was strange and definitely not what I was expecting. It left me unsettled and silent. But he just chuckled. "William. Call me Will." He reached for my hand and brought it up to his lips.

He paused, waiting, as if he wanted to gauge my reaction before kissing my hand. I could have sworn I stopped breathing. Until his skin touched mine. His lips were soft, but they left a trail of heat that shot up my arm and went straight to my core.

FUCK, this man was going to be hard to resist.

I heard myself giggle and shifted in my shoes as I tried to remove my hand from his grasp. I couldn't think when he touched me.
"Will? Nice to meet you, Will." I began feeling more stable with my hand stuffed in my pocket. "Listen, I didn't get a chance to tell you earlier, but it's been a long shift. I need some time to freshen up. My apartment is literally across the lane. It won't take long." I motioned behind him to my building.

"Of course." He answered quickly. "I should have realized. I'll walk you to your building and wait downstairs. Take all the time you need, Samantha."

My cheeks began to ache as I nodded. I felt both stupid and giddy at the same time. *Will*. Will was sophisticated and I was anything but.

We walked across the street together in silence. It was both awkward and lovely. When he offered me his arm, I didn't know what else to do but accept. It was formal and old-fashioned but I liked it. When we got to the door of the building, he stood aside after letting me in, but something didn't feel right to me. Maybe it was the way he made my head spin or maybe it was my racing heartbeat, but having him stand outside felt odd to me.

"You can come up and wait in my living room, if you'd like." I offered. A part of me knew that it was absolutely the wrong thing to do. I didn't know this guy from Adam, but there was something about him that made me feel like I could trust him.

The practical part of my brain screamed obscenities at me. Yet, despite opening myself up to becoming a real-life victim of a Law & Order episode, I pushed forward. I wasn't sure what made me do it. It could have been the way his pants seemed to be molded around his crotch and made my mouth water every time I glanced down. About a minute went by in silence. My hands got clammy and I could feel my brow furrow with the possibility that I had made a mistake.

Finally, he spoke. "Sounds good." He stepped through the doorway and placed his hand on my lower back as we walked to the elevators.

The ride up was quick and we both remained silent. His hand never moved from my back, though. In fact, it felt like it was burning a hole through my scrubs. Even with just a thin layer between our skin, his touch felt strong, possessive, and almost laced with desire. I felt drunk on this guy. I had to be careful.

Allison was out, which I knew she would be, so I showed Will to the couch and made a quick exit into my bedroom. Closing the door, I turned and leaned up against the back trying to stabilize myself. A couple of deep breaths later and I felt better. More controlled.

Alli and I shared a bathroom but it was a Jack and Jill, so we both had a door into our bedrooms. I silently thanked the contractors who built this place that I wouldn't have to run through the apartment wrapped in a towel.

I quickly jumped in the shower and washed off the grime of the day. Ten minutes later, I slapped on some mascara and lip gloss, a sundress, and some slides. At the last minute, I threw on a triple looped gold chain that sat delicately around my collarbone and hung down low on my chest. Catching sight of myself in the mirror, I paused. It was a mild improvement over the scrubs, but still as plain as ever. I couldn't understand why such a gorgeous man like Will was interested in a simple girl like me. But hey, he had seen me looking like shit already and he was now sitting in the adjoining room. Maybe there was hope for me yet.

With a deep breath, I opened my bedroom door and stepped out. He didn't miss a beat, up and on his feet in a second. Like he had been waiting, every second hoping that that would be the one when I emerged.

"You look beautiful." He murmured in a throaty rumble, low enough that I had to strain to hear him. For once, his words didn't faze me. It was always the first compliment men said. I knew he didn't mean it, but somehow the words still made me smile.

I hesitated, waiting for him to give me an indication of his next move. It was always better to wait and see what they wanted. But Will was different. He stared at me, really me. He locked onto my eyes and held me there. I waited for his gaze to meander lower, but it didn't. It had begun to feel like a staring contest, one that neither of us wanted to break.

But finally, I had to. "Uhm… shall we?" I asked hesitantly.
Instead of answering, he reached out and grabbed my hand. It felt small inside his larger one and he held it with a power and confidence that amazed but didn't leave me fearful. It was a new feeling for me - no fear. I couldn't think of time when I had ever felt that way.
My heart beat a little faster, and I was filled with hope thinking that perhaps this night would be different from all the rest.

His silence both intrigued me and enthralled me. Like a snake charmer, he kept me swaying in time to his magic and left me feeling like I was melting in his presence. Heat crept up my spine and across my chest. Butterflies fluttered in the pit of my stomach as he stared at me. And when he reached out and rested his hand on my shoulder, our skin touched and fire went shooting down my arm. Like a stab right into my heart, I was paralyzed.

"Will…I…Will?" I questioned.

He leaned down and the magnetic energy between us increased tenfold. A vein popped out on his neck and I could feel tingles all over my skin. Suddenly, the air seemed heavier. He was inches from my lips. I had to strain my neck to look up and as I did, those eyes. His eyes were a light blue that contrasted heavily with his dark hair. The stubble across his face cast a shadow, making his already sharp jawline even stronger.

His eyes locked on mine but still, he said nothing. I stumbled, lost my train of thought, and waited. He said nothing and did nothing but stare.

Until he didn't.

Chapter 16

Australia

Ashton Chase

"Stop. Talking." I growled.

I didn't wait for her answer. I couldn't. If I had to hear her call me Will again, I was going to scream. What had possessed me to say that? I didn't know. It wasn't a total lie, though. My full name was William Ashton Chase. It was just no one ever called me anything but Ash. William was my father. My asshole of a father who beat my mother and tried to burn down the shed with me inside it. I hated the name and hearing it on her lips when all I wanted was to hear my own name was both aggravating and painful. But I'd have to deal with it. I couldn't tell her that I'd lied. So instead, I went with what I knew and let desire guide me.

I was out of control. My heart and body were running the show and my brain was nowhere to be found. I watched as her breasts seemed to strain against the confines of her pretty sundress. I could see her nipples poking through and all I could think about was popping one in my mouth while my fingers played with the other until it stood at attention for me.

"Dr. Jordan, you are stunning." I breathed, inches from her lips. "I've wanted to kiss you since the first second I saw you outside the hospital."

I didn't wait for an answer. My lips crashed down on hers and the feeling was anything but what I expected. The sweet taste of her skin sent me barreling over the edge.

Aggressively, I pushed my tongue into her mouth, eager to explore every inch of it. I attacked her like I was starving and she responded in kind, melting into me and pressing her soft curves up against my chest and my cock.

Dragging my lips across her neck and down to her collarbone was like tasting heaven, but I already knew that it wasn't enough. I wanted to taste every goddam inch of her. I allowed myself to take little nips of her skin. Her little squeaks and moans encouraged me to slip the straps of the dress of her shoulders, exposing her bra and heaving breasts beneath it.

She was fumbling with the buttons on my shirt, but I pushed her away. That would come later. Now, I wanted to see and taste every last inch of this beautiful creature. Sliding my hands under her tiny frame, I lifted her up, her legs instinctively wrapping around my waist as I walked us back towards her couch.

"Is your roommate due back soon?" I mumbled between more fervent kisses. She shook her head as I crashed back into the pillows, pulling her on top of me. I was no longer thinking about dinner, or the name I had given her, my reputation, or even the promises that I had made to myself. Instead, I slid my hands under her dress and across her bare ass as I pulled her into me.

Her pretty perfect waves were starting to get tangled, her lip gloss was smeared across her cheek, and her dress was now hanging off of her in the most seductive way, showing everything and not enough at the same time. It was enough to drive a man wild.

"You look so fucking hot all messed up like this." I whispered as my thumb brushed across her swollen lips.

HEATWAVE

My hands slid up her body, taking her sundress with them. As she raised her arms, one pink nipple popped out from behind the lacy material of her bra. She was a vision and she was driving me wild. Just as I reached for that perfectly pink nipple with my mouth, I felt her small hands on my zipper.

"Ugh...Samantha..." I said, my voice hoarse with need.

"Wait..." I tried again. Not because I didn't want to feel her wrap those small hands around my swollen cock. No, it was more like I knew that if she did, it would be over. I would have her head down and ass up in seconds.

So instead, I sucked hard on her nipple and rolled it between my teeth, only stopping for a few seconds to whisper "I'd ask you how like this, Samantha, but your body has already told me everything I need to know." Her smile and innocent blush confirmed everything I needed to know.

"But the thing is, this is not enough for me. I can't wait to see that lovely pussy of yours. See if it's as pink as your nipples."

She nodded shyly.

"Stay still, angel." I told her as I pulled aside her panties and cupped her heated pussy.

"Swollen, wet, and bare...my favorite kind of pussy." I reveled in the fact that my words made her slightly uncomfortable. Nothing was hotter than a beautiful woman, visibly shamed from a little dirty talk. It was like a firecracker to my lust.

But my needs would have to wait, I wanted to please her first. My fingers slipped easily across her slick folds, making her moan and writhe in my lap. I kept distracting her by running my thumb over her swollen nub gently then circling harder and harder. I was mesmerized by her.

"You're so wet for me, angel." I growled. "Slick with need for my cock. I can't wait to be deep inside you, feeling every inch of you. Making you come undone and again and again for me."

With her moans getting louder, I wasn't sure she could even hear me.

"Samantha, I can be a rough lover. Do you understand? I don't do gentle."
"Will...I..." Her hesitation made me pause. *Will. What was I thinking?* Shit. She wasn't one of my London girls. I was taking this too far, too fast. I needed to backtrack.

"Say the word, Samantha, and I'll stop."

Except, she didn't have time to answer.

Suddenly, a rattling of keys could be heard at the front door.

"Fuck! It's Allison! My roommate!" Samantha screeched as she jumped off my lap and started rearranging herself. I, too, was up in a flash, adjusting myself.

"I thought you said she wasn't due home for hours!" I roared.

"Well, that's what I thought!" She barked back at me.

"Hey there..." Came a new voice directly behind me.

Allison. Well, this was a problem. The last thing I wanted was girl drama. I should have just taken her out for dinner like a gentleman. Instead, I let my cock think for me and now she was in a panic. I could have punched myself in the face for being so stupid.

HEATWAVE

"Hey Alli, sorry about this..." Samantha began to quickly make apologies.

She was blushing, obviously flustered and uncomfortable. I had done that. I had taken advantage of her and embarrassed her. *FUCK.*

"Don't worry about it. You okay, Sam?" Allison asked while eyeing me suspiciously. Clearly, she could see what I had just realized, too. I had to do something. Let Samantha save at least a little face.

"All good here. I was on my out anyway." I began, my palms raised as I walked to the door. "Samantha, my apologies. This was a mistake. It won't happen again." I continued, my voice now calm and under control. "Have a good night, ladies."

Her face began to crumble.

I closed the door with a feeling of emptiness in my stomach. It was over before it had begun. She was hurt and I had done that to her. I was an idiot. I didn't know how to date. I let lust take over and had embarrassed her in the process. However, it probably would have happened anyway. I supposed earlier was better than later and all that. Despite how she made me feel here in Australia, I would have hurt her when I returned to my life in London. Not to mention if I had tried to explain myself.

Who was I? A wealthy financial guru from London who moonlighted as a firefighter in Australia and lied to foreign girls just to get them into bed? Yeah, what a catch I was. Samantha Jordan was a special woman and I had treated her like a whore. No, actually, I treated the working girls in London better than that. At least I always made sure they got dinner first.

Chapter 17

Australia

Samantha Jordan

It was like being punched through the heart. A gaping wound had been opened and my insecurities were dripping out one by one. *How the hell had this happened?* But there was no need to search for an answer, I already knew. Cast aside just like all the times before. Who knows, maybe that had been his plan all along. Dinner was just an excuse, I suppose.

I had let this crazy chemistry between us over take my mind and my typically clear-headed reasoning. I had acted like every other stupid lust-crazed girl. How stupid of me. Fantasizing about him all day long. Why would I even think that a guy who kissed me before introducing himself would ever hold more possibility than a one-night stand? This was a new low. Even for me.

"Come on, honey, let's get you a drink." Allison wrapped her arm around me and brought me towards the couch. The fucking couch that I just been half naked on with Will's fingers up my pussy.

For the life of me, I couldn't understand what had just happened. Why had he said that this wouldn't happen again? Was he so embarrassed about Allison coming home that he wouldn't see me again? Or maybe making out with me wasn't as good for him as it was for me? Or maybe he just wanted a roll in the hay and couldn't be bothered to have to take me out to do it? Maybe it was all just one big excuse.

I was, for the first time ever, completely and utterly at a loss. Tears welled up behind my eyes as I tried to make sense of it all. *You just couldn't cut it, Sam.* The voice in my head began her incessant needling.

"I just don't get it, Alli!" I whined as she slid a glass of wine across the coffee table.

"Okay, start from the beginning! I need details." She said, chugging back a swig of beer.

"He just randomly showed up at the hospital this afternoon and asked me out. We were supposed to go for dinner. He picked me up after my shift, but I wanted to change, so we came here and he waited here while I went to change. Everything was fine at that point, he was interested, attentive even, his hand on my back as we walked. Easy conversation, I was truly excited about tonight. And…" I hesitated.

"I know we're still getting to know each other, Alli, but you have to understand. I NEVER date. I have some stuff that I'm working through, or trying to at least, but because of that, I just don't bother. I'm not interested. But Will, he was different! Something about him made me want to try…" I felt myself drift off as I thought about our first meeting.

"I knew you liked him, Sam. After he arrived at the hospital with Lucky, you talked about the hot firefighter for days."

"Yeah…" I trailed off, lost in thought.

"So, what went wrong? Did you guys even leave the apartment?" She asked.

"No, that's the thing. We didn't. All of a sudden, he kissed me, and it just went from there. We were all over each other. God, it was so hot. Passionate even…" I paused and giggled. "I don't even know how to describe how good it was!"

"And then it just wasn't. Just like that. It was as if all of a sudden, it was my fault and he just couldn't get out of here fast enough."

"Fuck, I'm sorry honey. Do you think it was my fault? I'm so sorry." Allison was so sweet for even asking, but of course that wasn't it.

"Absolutely not. I know something else was going on, I just don't know what it was."

Allison reached over and hugged me.

"I'm going to take a shower. Thanks for listening." I hugged her back.

It was only when I was safely in the bathroom that my emotions really hit. But the worst of it was the shame. Shame that I had let myself think that this time it would be different.

Why couldn't I have what everyone else seems to find so easily?

From Ava to Adriana and countless other friends along the way, everyone seemed to be able to find someone who loved them. Sure, some of those didn't make it past the beginning mark, but at least it was something. I felt like my whole life up to this point had been a charade. One that even my closest friends didn't fully understand.

Chapter 18

Australia

Ashton Chase

This was bullshit. It had been almost a week since our god-awful quasi date and I still couldn't get her out of my mind. I wanted to call and apologize, but any time I tried to piece together the words, they just didn't sound right. Pinching the bridge of my nose as I exited Jack's Uber, I took a deep breath before making my way back into the fire station yet again.

After being called back in early, Bradley had given me a couple of days off before my next shift. I probably should have figured things out with Samantha during that time, but it was too late. I now had another five days of work ahead of me. The fires had been raging harder this past week and the crew that was switching out was exhausted. They had worked longer hours than typical and were in for a much needed break. I welcomed the work, though. The past few days at the condo had been difficult. I spent time catching up with my London guys and working out. I'd even braved the dry heat for a couple more runs along Bondi Beach, but none of it soothed my mind. Even last night as I lay in bed, I'd been conflicted. I knew that I'd been an asshole, but I also felt strongly that I'd made the right choice.

Samantha was in a different category completely. Out of my league. A strong woman who knew what she wanted, successful in her own right, and passionate about her work. Someone like that didn't need a mental fuck up who was always hiding his past from the overbearing spotlight. Sure, I looked like I had it all together, but the reality was that I was living a lie. Whether it be here in Australia or even back in London, I wasn't really at home anywhere.

Not to mention that she had no clue about my real identity. But none of that stopped me from thinking about those soft brown eyes or her lush breasts that rose and fell with every breath. Her pert pink nipples that had elongated and hardened beneath my fingers or the way she had moaned when I slipped my hand between her legs. *Fuck!* Just remembering it now made me hard. I adjusted my pants and tried to put her out of mind. A week at the station would do me good.

"Ash!" Called out Bradley as he saw me approaching. "Damn, mate, I missed you! How was your time off?"

No choice but to play the game and laugh it off. "Decent. Got caught up on work, spent time in the gym. You know, the usual shit." I answered nonchalantly.

"Fuck that, mate! I want to know about your date!" He laughed as he punched my shoulder.

"My what…" I trailed off, taken aback for a second. Shit, I had completely forgotten that I had asked Bradley for restaurant recommendations.

"Yeah…um, sure. It was fine. Thanks." I answered casually, hoping he wouldn't press the issue more than that.

"Come on, man, you aren't getting away with that! Gimme details!" Bradley chuckled as he rubbed his hands together.

"Just wasn't what either of expected, I guess…" I mumbled, trying to come up with something that would get him off the topic. "Sorry mate, no second date!" I smiled as if I didn't give a shit.

HEATWAVE

"Aye, well, you're hangin' out with us boys for the next week, so we'll get you up and ready for round two."

"Done." I nodded in agreement. *Not a chance in hell.* I said silently to myself.

I needed to get back to my old ways. The ones that worked for me. Call up a service and have them send a girl according to my specifications. I could deal with that. No unnecessary talking, no fucking emotions, get what I needed and move on.

Samantha would never be like that. Not to me, anyway. She deserved better. Yet just as quickly as that thought entered my head, my blood began to boil. If she wasn't with me, she'd end up with someone else, and the thought of another man touching her filled me with rage. It was so confusing. For reasons I couldn't comprehend, this woman ignited emotions in me that were terrifying. I felt protective in a way that I never had about anyone, ever.

A few days of work to clear my head was what I needed.

I popped my head into the common room to say hello to the guys before dumping my stuff on the bed. We were having an early dinner before heading out for a night shift. Erik was in the kitchen making dinner, the smells coming from the kitchen just heavenly. We each had kitchen duty, but thankfully, mine wasn't until day three. I really wasn't much of a cook as I typically ordered everything back home. I did, however, have one specialty, my spaghetti sauce. It was a recipe that my foster mum had taught me. Memories of being in her kitchen and cooking with her floated back into my head. She had been good to me. The only woman who ever had.

Maybe if I managed to patch things up with Sam, I could have her over to the condo and make spaghetti for her...*FUCK! No! Stop thinking about her!* I scolded myself. Even if I did manage to get her to forgive me, I'd have so much explaining to do that I wasn't sure I would still be able to keep my reality a secret.

Chapter 19

Australia

Samantha Jordan

After that fateful night with Will, I tried to put it all behind me. In actuality, there really wasn't much to move forward from. Just intense chemistry followed by his weirdness before he ghosted me. But really, it was hardly ghosting when I had never even given him my number. *Although he did know where I worked and lived...*a little voice in my head always reminded me. *He could have tried.*

Fuck it. Stop thinking about him, Samantha! The sane part of my mind yelled back.

The sun peeked in from my curtains. I was warm and comfortable in my bed. I glanced at the clock and saw it was only 6:45am. I still had an hour before I needed to clock in to the hospital. And being that it was literally across the street, maybe I had time to take a late morning…

My hand slid down my body and between my legs as thoughts of Will's hard, muscular chest entered my mind. I'd actually been thinking about him all night as I drifted in and out of dreams about the way he had kissed me with such passion. It was hard to imagine that he kissed everyone like that. It had seemed so personal, so special, as if we had something between us that was unique.

With one hand gently pushing apart the folds between my legs and the other beginning to twist my nipples, I allowed my mind to fill with memories of that unfinished night. Goosebumps prickled across my skin as thoughts of him invaded my mind.

"Are you wet for me already, my angel?" his husky voice demanded in my head.

I giggled at the slight embarrassment the words caused me.

"Maybe. You do things to me…" I trailed off, only slightly aware that I was having a conversation with a real man, inside the fictional fantasies of my mind.

"You like it when I make you blush, don't you, you dirty girl?" He pressed on, his fingers having found my heated core and swirling his fingers around the tiny nub of nerve endings that were now on fire.

"Fuck! Will…yes…please!" I begged shamelessly to the invisible man in my mind.

"Not so fast, angel. I'll be the one to tell you when you get to come." He whispered darkly, his breath in my ear making my head spin.

Even in my fantasies, he was everything I had ever wanted in a man. Sex had never been as exciting as I wanted it to be. It was something I did to keep boyfriends happy and make it seem like I was the same as everyone else. But reality was that I was afraid to ask for what I really wanted. A man I trusted enough to let my guard down with. Someone who would take control of my body but only because I let him. In just those few moments with Will, he had made it seem like all of that could be more than just a fantasy.

Chapter 20

Australia

Ashton Chase

I stumbled into the fire house dazed and confused from the smoke inhalation. This last trip out to the bush had been almost impossible. And the most depressing. It was a community in despair. Almost every home in the area had either been totally destroyed or ruined enough that it was unlivable.

We had evacuated the town overnight. Knocking on doors, dragging people from their beds. Some had come running out into the streets, screaming in panic about their children, elderly grandparents, and even pets that were lost or still stuck inside their homes. We had gone in and pulled them out one by one.

For the most part, I had kept my cool, but there had been one moment that nearly did me in. I had been in a small bungalow searching for a toddler. His parents had run from the house when they couldn't find him in his room. Their smoke alarm had gone off and they ran to get him, but when they didn't find him in his crib, they had run out into the streets in despair. I heard the mother wailing before I saw her and I knew that sound. Brought me right back to when I had been inside the shed at five years old. That vision of a locked wooden door and hearing my mother scream on the other side was something that would be locked inside my mind forever. Except this time, I wasn't locked inside by a maniacal father. I was a grown man who could change the course of this child's fate if I intervened in time. That was motivation like none other for me. I drew up my hose and ran inside the burning building.

His name was Ryan and I called for him in every smoke-filled room, closet, and under each bed. It was a small home and only one floor so when I didn't find him after three rounds, I began to get nervous. The smoke was getting thicker and the hose began to feel heavier on my back so I set it down. Where was this child? Was he hiding in a cupboard maybe? Sometimes small kids in the throes of fear would act like animals and go into hiding. It had happened many times. Then I heard the sound, the sound of wood crashing. I looked up and for a split second, I envisioned the same accident that had happened in London.

"Noooo!" I heard myself scream as I darted out of the way. *Crash!* It obliterated the floor and went straight through to the foundation as it crashed down.

"Ash? Ash!" I heard Bradley calling my name. "The boy is outside! He ran out the back, come out man!"

Slowly and carefully, I picked myself up and crawled to the front door. My lungs heaved and gasped for air as pain seared through my body and sweat dripped into my eyes.

But I saw him. Ryan was there and he was in the arms of his parents. Tears pricked the back of my eyes but this time it was not from the smoke. Seeing the family together was all I could ask for.

I couldn't revel in it for too long, though. There was too much work to be done here. Too many to save. But save we did. We worked for hours until the entire town was safe.

We worked like that for days. The same routine. Work, then back to the firehouse, eat, rest, and do it again. I mostly kept to myself at the station. Many of the guys liked to let off steam by playing cards, chatting, and socializing. But that wasn't for me. I worked out and slept.

The first few days I was so tired that even if I had the words to speak to Samantha, I wouldn't have been able to call her. Not that I knew her number. Fuck, I had really gone about this all wrong. I was going to have to turn it around. I needed to. I wasn't sure I could stop thinking about her. She was always in my head, her scent sweet and fresh but also deeply sensual. She had invaded my thoughts and my dreams. At night, alone in that awful firehouse cot, I thought about having her naked in my arms, walking along the beach with her, and even having her all to myself to savour all night long.

I even envisioned being back in London with her. Yes, London. I had been wrong to deny my obvious feelings. She wasn't like anyone else. She wasn't someone I could walk away from. In the short amount of time we had spent together, she had invaded every part of me, body, mind, and soul. I wanted her today, tomorrow, and back in London.

But none of that could happen if I didn't fix this fuck up.

On the last night of my week at the station, my phone buzzed in my pocket. Typically, I didn't answer it at the station, but I glanced over and saw that it was Daniel, my top broker and leader of my team.

"Dan! How's it going, mate?" I answered quickly. I had given specific instructions not to bother me during station time, so I knew that if he was calling it was important.

"Ash! Sorry to bother you, man, but I had no choice." He apologized.

"It's okay, tell me what's happening."

First, he gave me a run-down of clients and numbers. Thankfully, everything was on track as it had been the last time we spoke. "So, what's the emergency then, Dan?" I asked. "Everything seems fine."

"You're right, it is, but I was actually calling because there's an event that you've been invited to. Actually, the entire team has been invited, and honestly, this could be really great publicity for all of us." Dan began.

I sighed. This was the type of shit that I wished I could ignore. Public events were not my thing. In fact, I aimed to avoid them like the plague. However, I had a lot of high-profile clients that felt it necessary to invite me to their personal and public events. All for good causes, things like charity events and such. But it just wasn't my scene. I hated the press and their constant barrage of questions, forever prying into my life, and trying to find small amounts of dirt they could enhance.

"Come on, Ash…" Pressed Dan. "It's Fredrick Layton who invited us and the thing is…this could be your chance to actually have a conversation with him."

Dan knew that I had been trying to get Layton to invest with us for over a year. To say the man was eccentric was an understatement. He had rebuffed all of our attempts for a meeting. His office told us that he did not meet with just anyone. In fact, in order to get to Layton, you had to prove yourself worthy enough by your success rate. If and when he deigned you worthy, you would get an invite to a private affair at his London estate.

This was literally the moment I had been waiting over a year for. And somehow as Murphy's law would have it, I was thousands of miles away in Australia playing volunteer fireman and obsessing over a girl I barely knew.

"The team needs you at the helm on this one, Ash. You need to come home." Cautioned Dan as if he could see my internal dialogue.

Fuck it. "You're right, Dan. This is huge. Okay, let me organize things here and I'll figure it out. When's the party?"

"Saturday." Dan's tone was hesitant.

"Shit! Saturday? That's literally in four days! Why are you only telling me now?" I barked into the phone.

"Because we just got the invite, you ass! You know what he's like! Layton expects you to drop everything and be there." *Dammit.* I had forgotten about Layton's obsession with constantly making you prove you wanted it.

I ran my soot filled hands through my hair. "Okay, I'll figure it out. Call you when I land."

I needed to speak to Bradley. I hated breaking my word with him but I had no choice. I wouldn't be gone for long, though. Just the weekend and then I'd be back to finish up here.

Also, I had to buck up and go find Samantha. I had just three days to make things right if there was any hope of returning to her after London.

I picked up my phone and called the vet hospital.

"NSW Sydney Animal Clinic!" Answered a perky voice through my earbuds.

"Hello there, can you tell me if Dr. Jordan is working tonight?"

Chapter 21

Australia

Samantha Jordan

My pager had been beeping incessantly all night long. Although I wasn't technically working, being on call in the middle of raging bushfires was pretty much making it just the same.

"Are you sure you don't need me to come in?" I asked my colleague on the other end of the line for the third time that evening. "Seriously, all I'm doing is sitting on my couch scrolling through my phone." *And dreaming about Will,* my mind whispered.

It had been over a week since our date night gone wrong and even though I was certain I wouldn't hear from him again, I couldn't seem to control my mind. I dreamt about his hands on my body, his tongue in my mouth, and his voice whispering dirty things in my ear. It was an all-consuming distraction.

"No need, Dr. Jordan, just need a quick consult on the joey issue." Answered Rachel, the vet technician.

We had fifty orphaned joeys that were in makeshift pouches. Typically, a joey would leave the pouch at about eight months, but prior to that, they enjoyed hopping in and out to look around and explore. Most of the ones we had were pretty much still in their pouches as they were recovering from being badly burned. However, we did have a handful whose injuries were less severe, and they had been hopping out and wanting to explore. Unfortunately for them, we just didn't have the room for them to do so, not to mention that exploring an ER was not joey proof.

"I've reached out to some of the local sanctuaries and one them said they would drop by in the morning. Hopefully, they will have room to take most of the feisty ones. They're pretty much ready to go anyway, maybe just a few with antibiotics to take for a few more days." I told Rachel.

"Okay, that sounds great because this is crazy here!" She laughed. "Not joking, a joey just found his way to the front waiting room!"

I started to laugh. "This is good! This is what we want."

I smiled to myself. This was the reason I had come to Australia. I wanted to make a difference, and we were finally starting to have some good moments where I felt that we were moving in the right direction.

"What about Lucky?" I asked. The entire staff knew him by name. He was the little orphaned koala cub that Will had brought in. I would have had a soft spot for him anyway, but the fact he was the reason I had met Will? Well, his presence was somewhat bittersweet.

"He's doing just fine." I could hear Rachel smiling as she spoke. "I'm going to miss him, though."

"Same here. Wish he could hang out with us a little longer." I answered softly.

Tomorrow, Lucky would be heading out to a sanctuary with the others. Maybe without him at the clinic, I'd be able to stop obsessing over Will.

Chapter 22

Australia

Ashton Chase

After finding out that she would be back at work tomorrow, I knew what I needed to do.

"Brad!" I called down to my friend who was chatting with the guys in the common room. "Need to talk to you, my friend." I continued as I made my way down the stairs.

Brad must have understood the tone of my voice because he was up and coming towards me just as quick as I had come down. We moved off into the hallway outside the common room.

"Okay, first off, I'm going to have head back to London for a few days. I …"

"Days? Shit, you must like the jet set life." He laughed. "Where to after that?"

I gave him a blank look. "Here, mate, I'll be coming back here."

"No need, Ash. Honestly, I was going to tell you after this shift that we're doing much better now and I think that if you need to get back to work, we've got things covered. The fires seem to be dying down and I think, although it might be too early to tell, but I think that we might finally be moving in the right direction."

"Really?" I took his words in. "Because this last mission was brutal."

"You're right, it was. However, they're getting fewer and fewer and we have a new crew due to arrive next week."

This changed everything. My timeline was already uncertain and if Bradley didn't think he needed me anymore... what did that mean for Samantha?

I had to move fast if I wanted a chance with her.

"Umm, okay. Well, I had meant to return but let's see what happens, okay? If you need me, I'm here for you. Coming here was important to me and I'm not bailing on you or the guys. I just have to take care of something in London that needs my attention that I've been neglecting."

"Totally understand, my friend. Let's keep each other posted and take things as they come." Bradley reached out, grabbed my shoulder, and pulled me into a bear hug. I let him, but it felt awkward to me. I had never been all that great at friendship or any signs of affection.

I packed up my stuff and made my way down to the rec room to talk to the guys. "I'll be heading out for a little while, guys. I have to go home and take care of some stuff. But Bradley here said he would stay in contact and keep me abreast of the situation out here. I want you to know that I will be back as soon as I can if you feel I'm needed here."

"Thanks for everything, man, you've been a huge help." Called out someone in the back of the group.

"Yes, agreed mate, it's been a pleasure!" said another.

HEATWAVE

I called for Jack and when he came, I raised my hand one final time to the station guys as the car pulled away. A sense of relief and calmness came over me as I thought of all the experiences; Lucky the koala, the hundreds of people and animals that we had evacuated. I had done what I had come here to do, but if they needed me, I'd be back.

In the meantime, I had a new fire to put out.

****

When I walked into the ER the next morning, there was a very different vibe in the place. The last few times, it had been mad chaos. People running everywhere, animal sounds coming from every corner, animals being housed in the front lobby. It had been an absolute war zone. Today though, it was calmer. More organized.

I had chosen a pair of shorts and a plain white t-shirt, unassuming casual and non-threatening. Hopefully, it would help me.

"Could you page Dr. Jordan, please?" I asked the girl at the front desk.

She gasped, frozen for a moment like she had seen a ghost, then a small smirk spread across her face. "Are you from London? Has anyone ever told you that you look like…"

"Pardon me?" I was taken aback at her question.

"Sorry." She flushed. "You just seem familiar to me."

So much for being incognito. But I smiled and nodded in appreciation.

Chapter 23

Australia

Samantha Jordan

When I went in to work that day, the last person I expected to see was HIM.

It wasn't often that I was called to the front desk, and I had a ton of paperwork.

"What's up, Cynthia? I ..." My voice trailed off as I saw him. He was so big he practically filled the glass doorway behind him. His dark brown hair was slightly messed up, his skin more golden than the last time I saw him. He looked like a Greek god, but it was his eyes, boring through me like a raging fire, igniting every possible nerve ending in my body.

"Samantha." His voice, calm and deep, rattled my nerves. Papers fell from my hands and I nervously scrambled to pick them up.

"I've got them." His deep gravelly voice said as a thick bicep pulled me from my knees.

"Will, I ...what are you doing here?" I asked, trying not to look as flustered as I felt.

"Waiting for you." He stared again. Damn that strong silent type, I literally had no idea what he was thinking. Was he really here to see me? Or maybe someone else? After the way he had left my apartment, I couldn't imagine that this was really about me.

"I owe you an apology, Samantha."

Suspicion flooded my mind. Unlike him, though, silence wasn't my forte. Snarky was.

"No shit, Sherlock!" I raised my voice at him then quickly tried to reign it in as I felt eyes on us. "You ran hot and cold in an instant last time." I paused for effect.

"What the hell happened?" I continued, softer this time.

He looked at me and despite the hard lines of his face, his eyes had softened. "I panicked and made a bad choice. But I haven't stopped thinking about you since. Please let me take you out properly this time."

Fuck. How could I say no to that? Plus, I couldn't deny that he smelled amazing. My heart literally skipped a beat every time he smiled.

He reached over and lifted my chin up to face him. "When I tell you that you are all I have thought about since the last time I saw you, it's true. Every time I walked in to a fire zone, every time I evacuated a family, every time I found another helpless life, I thought of you, Samantha Jordan."

This man. His words were enough to make me melt.

My mind was firing off every excuse in the world why this was a bad idea, but my heart kept pushing me to ignore it. And my body, well…she had abandoned all sense of reason the first time this beautifully dangerous man had walked into my field of vision.

"Okay… I'll go out with you again, but this time, it's on my terms." I laughed, feeling him melt my walls.

"Only this time, angel." I could have sworn that he growled.

I giggled nervously. "Give me your number." I said, pulling out my phone. He recited the numbers and I punched them into my phone.

It rang and he smiled. "Now I won't have to track you down ever again." He said darkly as I shivered.

"How about lunch tomorrow?" I could have offered sooner but I didn't want to make it easy for him. Yes, I was excited to try it again but at the same time, wary. Always wary. After all, up till now, Will had been like every other man I'd ever met.

Except he wasn't, whispered my heart.

You think he gives a shit, Samantha? Ha. He's back to get the fuck he missed out on last time. Just watch, you'll see.

Will's voice interrupted the argument in my head. "I'll call you tonight."

I nodded and tried to step back but not before he had grabbed my wrists firmly, making me gasp. Fear coursed through me, but he didn't move. He held me there and stared into my eyes, making me forget all the warnings bells that were detonating inside my head.

"Yes…" I nodded. And when I did, he released my hands.

I stood there in a daze as he walked out the door. *What the hell had I just agreed to?* Shaking my head, I began to make my way back to the tiny office and the mountain of paperwork that was waiting for me there when I heard my name being called once again.

"Dr. Jordan? Dr. Jordan?"

"Yes?" I turned to see our floor coordinator waving at me. "Dr. Joel wanted me to tell you that two of your colleagues from America will be joining you here tomorrow!"

That stopped me dead in my tracks. "What do you mean?" I asked, slowly turning my head.

"Dr. Dave Watson and Dr. Ann-Marie Legare!" She said, a huge smile on her face.

A shudder ran through me at lightning speed. *Dave was coming. HERE? What the hell kind of shit show was this about to turn in to?*

Chapter 24

Australia

Ashton Chase

I couldn't wait to call her that evening. I couldn't believe my good luck that she had accepted my apology. I knew that she had every right to rebuff me and yet she hadn't. In fact, I could have sworn she was happy to see me. Fuck that, I knew she had been. That pert little mouth, the way she chewed her bottom lip as she dropped the papers. Seeing her bent over like that, all flustered, had done things to me. My cock had been rock hard the entire time she had been close to me. And even now as I lay in my bed thinking about her and stroking my cock, she was the reason for it.

"Hello?" her soft, gentle voice came through the speakers and into my head.

"Hello, Samantha. Just wanted to check in with you."

"Mmm…kay?" She questioned.

"How was the rest of your shift?" I hated small talk and knew I'd run out of things to say soon.

"It was okay. Not as interesting as when you were there, though." Her breathy voice floated through the phone.

That took me by surprise. What was she doing? I absentmindedly stroked myself, hardening even more with every word she said. I imagined her next to me in my bed, telling me about her day. The things I would do to her…

Although I had intended to be an honorable gentleman, the suggestive way she spoke to me had me veering off-track in seconds.

"Angel…would you do something for me?" I asked, giving in to my lustful thoughts once again.

"Sure, Will. What is it?" I winced at the name. Why had I been so stupid? I fucking hated hearing it. I cursed my tainted past for fucking me up. I longed to hear her breathe my name, scream it as I pleasured her. Just the idea of hearing my name on her lips was erotic to me. Protecting my identity had gone too far. I would have to rectify it. But not now. In person. Now there was something else I wanted much more.

I pressed the Facetime button and waited for her to accept. A second passed but she did it. *Good girl.*

She came into view and I felt my heart skip a beat. She was curled up on the couch, the very same couch that I kissed her on, the same couch where she had let me see and touch the most intimate part of her. Dammit. I felt my muscles contracting. I was careful to hold the phone up to my face as my other hand was still deep in my shorts.

"I wanted to see you." I growled at her.

She giggled and waved. "Hey! Here I am."

Once again, I made a split-second pivot. Pushing aside my desire to know her more intimately, I changed course. The energy between us felt explosive, but it was more than lust. I felt something, something I hadn't in a long time, and I couldn't understand why. I needed to know more about her, to understand who she was and why she affected me so.

"Last time, we didn't talk much." I began. "Not that I minded…" I trailed off and watched her breasts rise as she took a deep breath and remembered.

"I want to start over with you, know who you are, Samantha. I need to do this before I see you and get distracted by that sexy little mouth of yours."

I paused and she brushed a strand of hair from her eyes. She looked down then up again.

"Tell me why you came to Australia."

"Okay…" She hesitated.

Over an hour later, I had heard her story, and the connection between us was even deeper. I respected her deep love for this country and her desire to help those who were in dire need. The most basic of things that we could have together was there. The tightness in my chest intensified. This woman was special.

Time passed as we spoke. I tried to be as honest as I could. I wanted to tell her my name, I really did. I started a few times, then backtracked. It just didn't seem like the right time to mention it, especially as it was technically our first real honest conversation. Honest…well, as much as it could have been.

***

The next day, I stood outside her building and took a deep breath before ringing her flat. I hated this building. With the dirty back alleyway and all kinds of people going in and out, it just wasn't safe. I thought about having her at the condo with me, but I knew it was too soon. Maybe she would agree to stay there while I went to London, though. *Fuck, London!* I hadn't mentioned that to her. Add it to my growing list of things I'd avoided talking about.

"Coming down!" She called through the intercom. I chuckled. Guess she wasn't going to risk having me come up to her place a second time. I suppose I couldn't blame her for that. I really had made an ass of myself. Tonight would be different, though. It would be classy and special and just like her. The door opened and she was a vision.

"Hey, Will." Her breathy voice floated towards me and I watched as she chewed on her pouty bottom lip.

Control, Ash. Stay in control.

"You look beautiful, angel." I said as I inhaled that sweet scent that was uniquely Samantha Jordan. She smiled and then twirled around. Her reaction caught me off guard. Her pretty little sundress showed off her golden tan and toned legs. A vision.

"Perfection." I growled as I grabbed her and pulled her in to my face. I held off for a second to watch her reaction. Her breath hitched as she looked up at me.

"Glad you like." She smiled, but her playfulness was gone. Something had changed when I grabbed her.

I leaned in and waited but she didn't move. I hesitated.

"What are you feeling, Samantha?" I asked.

She looked down and mumbled something that I didn't catch.

"Words, angel, speak clearly. I asked you what you were feeling." I pressed as I raised her face to meet my eyes.

"I don't know…" She faltered.

"Sure, you do, Samantha. Tell me." I pressed again.

"You just surprised me when you grabbed me. And well…I guess, I'm remembering when you kissed me last time. I don't want the night to end like that again."

I sighed. I still had work to do.

"I hear you, angel. And I promise you that it won't. Not this time." I could only hope she heard the sincerity in my voice.

"Do you feel it between us, angel? That pull of electricity? We can't deny it. And mark my words, I will kiss you tonight. But not until after I take you out. We're going for dinner, drinks, a walk along the beach, but when it's over, know that I will kiss you. If, of course, you still want me to."

She swallowed and the corners of her mouth turned up. Her smile said that she knew full well that I wanted to do much more than just kiss her tonight.

Chapter 25

Australia

Samantha Jordan

I will not sleep with him tonight. I will not sleep with him tonight.

Like a mantra, I tried to keep repeating the words in my head, but it was useless. My body had betrayed me within two minutes of being in his presence. His masculine scent enveloped my senses, making my body quiver in anticipation. But it wasn't just lust, it seemed like I had known this man my whole life.

We'd bonded over so much, but there was also something that made me uneasy. Every time I said his name, his expression changed. To what, I wasn't sure…but there was definitely something there. Or when I asked him about his life in London, the way he brushed me off was just…well, odd.

It was like he was hiding something, but I wasn't sure what it could be. He seemed like a stand-up guy. A fitness trainer, and obviously a good one by that killer body, and a part time firefighter. A selfless man who cared for others. Yet still, my suspicions were on high alert.

He took me to a little bistro in the heart of the city, right under the Sydney Harbour Bridge. It was a quaint little spot with a terrace and views of the Sydney Opera House. We could smell the salt in the air and with the sun setting across the water, it felt perfectly romantic.

"How is work?" He asked as he held my hand in his.

His question immediately had the hair on my neck stand up as I remembered Dave. *Fuck*. He was supposed to show up soon and I still had no idea how he had managed it. But I wasn't going to think about that tonight. No, tonight was Will and I. We were finally smoothing things out and having a good time. Tonight was not the night to bring up shit from home.

"Great. I wish I could stay for longer…" I trailed off because I didn't want this to get weird. I only had another month left before I was due to fly home. I also had no idea about Will's plans.

"Let's not talk about home tonight, let's just enjoy this night as if we have every other night in front of us." He said, looking deep into my eyes as if he was reading my mind.

I sucked in air at the sound of his words as tears pricked the back of my eyes. I nodded. He was absolutely right. So why was I fighting tears? What was wrong with me?

Thankfully, the waiter chose that moment to return and set down our order. Immediately, my mouth watered. Fresh seafood was my kryptonite. The Australian prawn risotto and Sydney rock oysters that we had ordered looked and smelled incredible.

"Can I make a suggestion?" The waiter asked.

"Absolutely." Will answered.

"Rock oysters have a creamy, rich flavour. They are best paired with a Champagne. Preferably a full-bodied one that leaves a fruity sweetness on the palate." He answered.

"Done! Bring it on over, please." Smiled Will.

HEATWAVE

"No really!" I protested. "Please, Will, Champagne is expensive and I'm not even sure I will like it."

He just smiled at me. "Don't worry about it. And, I'm sure you'll love it."

As it turned out, he was right. The food and the Champagne were an incredible combination. We ate, drank, and laughed. God, he made me laugh. That evening was like no date I had ever been on. By the time we had finished, I was relaxed, happy, and completely drunk on his presence.

"Let's go for a walk." Will said as he grabbed my hand and led me from the restaurant after paying the bill. The sun was setting and the heat was slowly beginning to subside as he wrapped his arm around me and held me close. I was starting to like this feeling of being small and protected next to him.

"Will, this has been a really nice evening." I began, smiling up at him as we stepped on to the pathway that led under the bridge.

Suddenly, he stopped short and turned to face me. Creases around his eyes appeared as a look of concern shadowed his face.

"Samantha, I need to tell you something…and I've been avoiding it all night." He began, his voice slightly cracking.

I felt my chest tighten. Not again…"Will…what do you mean?"

Adrenaline shot through me as we both paused and stared. *Here we go again,* began the voice…*Did you actually think this would be a fairy tale? You're so gullible.* She cackled in my ear.

Squeezing my eyes shut, I pushed away her voice. No, not this time, whatever it was, it would be okay.

"Just say it, Will. I can't take the suspense. And just so you know, this really sucks because I was having a great time." I heard the crack in my voice and swallowed hard to push down the lump that was threatening to overpower me.

"Me too, Samantha, and that's why it's now or never. And I'm sorry, please know that I didn't mean to lie to you." Will said softly.

Oh, Fuck.

He sighed and stepped back, releasing my hands. Running his hands through his hair, I watched the conflict take hold of him and wondered what he could have possibly lied about. We barely spoke the first time we had gone out, our phone conversation had gone well, and tonight had been perfect. *Almost.* Something just didn't make sense.

"Okay, so here's the thing, Samantha." He was pacing up and down the cobblestone pathway. Finally, he grabbed my hand again and pulled me to a nearby bench.

As we sat down, he spoke. "I understand if this upsets you, but I can't bear to hear you say Will one more time."

My eyebrows shot up in surprise. "Excuse me?"

"My full name is William Ashton, but everyone calls me Ashton or Ash. William was my father's name and well, I didn't have the best relationship with him, so hearing his name is not something I enjoy." He was beginning to ramble but it didn't matter, I couldn't control myself.

I laughed.

I laughed so fucking hard that my eyes began to tear up. Within seconds, I was full blown crying and hysterically laughing at the same time. Then I noticed.

He was staring at me blankly.

"Why the hell did you tell me your name was Will then?" I said between chuckles as I grabbed his hand and held it in mine.

"I don't know…" He said slowly, still staring at me like I was crazy. "I guess I was nervous?" He took a deep breath.

"Samantha, you do things to me that no one else has ever done. When I look at you, I want to both eat you alive and take care of and protect you. I'm so confused and that's new for me because I'm always in control of myself."

"I hear you…these feelings are new for me too, Wi…Ashton." I quickly corrected myself.

He smiled. Damn that was an electric smile.

"Honestly, you didn't need to be so worried about your name. You could have just casually mentioned it. It's hardly a lie." His smile was starting to fade and I wanted it back. "Besides, I like the name Ashton better. It suits you!" I leaned over and kissed his lips gently.

For a split second, he didn't move. He let my lips graze his without returning the kiss. But it was all of two seconds before he mauled me, grabbing the back of my head and sucking me into his vortex. I had already been teetering on the edge of desire all night, but when his tongue found its way into my mouth, I lost all sense of reason. I was his.

We inhaled each other and between fervent kisses, he whispered, "Come back to my place, Samantha."

It wasn't a question, more like a statement, but I didn't care. Somehow, everything just felt different with this man. The name thing was kind of odd, but I didn't want anything to ruin this almost perfect night. I pushed away any doubts that were left and for the first time in a long time, I listened to my heart instead of my mind.

Chapter 26

Australia

Ashton Chase

I wasn't wasting another fucking second under that bridge. I needed to hear her scream my name, my real fucking name. Her breathy moans as I kissed her already had me harder than ever. We needed privacy and we needed it now.

As we sat in the back of the Uber, she cuddled into me. With one arm wrapped around her shoulders, I let my other hand rest on her bare thigh as my lips grazed her forehead. Slowly, I slid my hand up her leg. She looked up at me beneath those beautiful, thick lashes, her eyes wide with surprise. I smirked and gave her a wink. Her warm, soft skin trembled beneath my touch. Leaning down, I whispered in her ear. "Open your thighs, angel." My fingers reached up and stroked her through her panties.

"Please, you can't…" She protested from under heavy-lidded eyes.

I chuckled and kissed her forehead. "Want me to stop?"

"Fuck no, but…" She looked nervously at the back of the driver's head.

"Let me worry about that." I reassured her. Keeping my eyes forward on the driver, I let my fingers explore. Her hand tightened around the sleeve of my shirt as her back arched, pushing her breasts out even more. Fuck, I couldn't wait to get those beauties back in my mouth again. My cock was already busting through my pants when she gently covered the bulge with her hand.

I smiled. "Put that hand away, angel. This is about you."

"You're no fun, Ash."

God. My name on her lips was like magic to my soul. I was going to devour this girl.

Chapter 27

Australia

Samantha Jordan

Up and down he slid that finger, tickling me through the fine fabric of my panties, teasing me into a state I had never felt before. For all the times I had been with guys, it had never felt like this. Foreplay had barely worked and I usually either panicked and ruined the moment or felt nothing at all. Yet here we were in the back of a car, and this guy had me writhing with more desire than I had ever felt in the company of another person. It felt so intimate, so trusting, and so fucking good.

By the time we arrived at his place, I was ready to beg him to fuck me.

He looked completely unaffected. He got out, opened the door for me, and offered his hand to steady me as I stepped out. It was like being with the hottest Prince Charming ever.

"Sorry, you have me a little worked up." I giggled as I hung on to him.

"That's perfect. I want you like that all the time." Ash answered as he led me inside.

I had to tell him. There was still a chance that I'd panic and I didn't want to ruin what we had.

"Yeah so, it's important that you know something." I started.

We stopped in his front entrance.

"What is it, angel?" His eyes looked at me with concern.

"I love being with you and I love how you make me feel, but there's a chance if we continue that I might panic, or zone out at some point."

He just stared.

"I have...triggers, I guess. I'd rather not go into it more, but just so you know...Anyway, I'm sure I'll be fine." Backtracking was easier than saying any more. I was sweating. Shit that was hard.

Ashton didn't say anything, he just nodded and brushed his thumb across my cheek before pulling me close and kissing the top of my head. There was something about his reaction that softened me. Made me calmer. It was like he understood trauma even if he didn't know the details.

We stood like that for a few minutes before he spoke. "Would you like a tour?" he asked.
I nodded, not trusting my voice.

He took my hand and led me in.

The condo was beautiful. Huge rooms, stunning décor, views that over-looked Bondi Beach.

"So, this where I've been staying." He spoke as he led me through the garden pathway to the blue front door.

This is incredible! This sure beats my shitty place." I laughed. "I shouldn't complain though, it's free."

"Well, this is actually Bradley's Air BnB, and he's been generous enough to let me use it while I'm here. Apparently, tourist season is a bit low this year." He had a twinkle in his eye, making me laugh.

"That's an awful joke but it is kind of funny." I giggled.

"Drink?" He asked as he walked to the bar.

"Yes, please!" I sighed with relief.

"What's your pleasure, Madame?" Ash smiled at me.

"Any chance you can make me an Aperol spritz?" I asked, reaching up on my toes to look over the bar.

"At your service, angel." As Ashton made the drinks, I walked around the place, taking it all in. The condo gave me a different view of Australia. More of a holiday feel. I could see how people wanted to vacation here. The condo was mostly white with a beach theme. Dried starfish and coral paintings of the bluest water I had ever seen graced the walls.

Turns out Ashton was quite the barman. "Mmm, this is so good!" I exclaimed. The flavors swirled in my mouth before I swallowed them.

"Only one, angel. I need you focused tonight…" Ashton's words trailed off as he took the glass from my hand as I finished off the last sip.

I shuddered with need as he reached for the hem of my dress and lifted it above my head.

"So beautiful…" His words trailed off as his hands took over.

"You're shaking, angel…"

Standing there in nothing but my bra and panties, I felt raw, exposed, but something else, too. Something I had never felt before…trust.

"Don't worry, angel. I know all about triggers. We can work through them together." Ash whispered as he wrapped his arms around me.

"I trust you, Ash, and I've never wanted anyone the way I want you now."

That was all it took.

He scooped me up and marched me into his bedroom, all while devouring my mouth like he was starving. His hands were everywhere, stripping what was left of my clothing and making me tremble with need. Ash had me naked and splayed out on his bed in a matter of seconds.

"Baby, you're so beautiful, I want to taste every part of you." He murmured as his lips left a trail of kisses along my jawline. He made his way down to the soft flesh of my neck and began to gently nip at the delicate skin. While his mouth was gentle, his hands were not. Fingers found my nipples and a tentative pull turned to harder twisting and rolling in a matter of seconds. It was like he was perfectly in tune to my body before I was. He anticipated my reactions and gave me what I craved before I even knew I craved it.

"How…how do you know?" I asked breathlessly as his hand slipped between my legs and began gently circling the swollen flesh.

"Know what, sweetheart?" he answered.

How had I never felt like this before? I had boyfriends and plenty of casual hookups, but none had ever left me a panting, naked mess like I was in that moment. Like I had been the first time at my apartment. This man was different. He made me different, made me feel things I never had. And I wanted more. Fuck, I wanted more.

The words tumbled out of my mouth. "How to…make me feel?"

It's funny how sometimes things are okay in your head, but as soon as they are let out into the world, everything begins to crumble. My words suddenly had a power that I hadn't been aware of. They released a darkness that had been hiding so quietly, even I hadn't noticed. Churning began in the pit of my stomach, sending an uneasiness throughout my body. Suddenly nausea came over me and I felt myself retreating into the darkness of my mind.

Ash seemed to notice that I had gone into my head. "Angel? Stay with me, angel, okay?"

CASSIDY LONDON

Chapter 28

Australia

Ashton Chase

One minute she had been right there in the moment with me and the next she was gone. Retreating into her head. I could see it happening and felt powerless to stop it.

"Samantha? Take some deep breaths." I sat her up and coached her through a few. As her breath steadied, I asked again. "You started disappearing, what happened?" I held her hands in mine and waited. She needed time. I knew these things couldn't be rushed.

"I'm sorry, I'm so sorry." She was tearing up and shaking.

"Can I hold you?" I asked, my arms open. She nodded quietly. We sat like that for what seemed like forever. Just as I was about to suggest we move to the couch, she spoke.

"It's not a pretty story..." she began.

There's only one answer when someone offers to show the deepest part of themselves. "I'll listen anyway."

***

I had assumed a bit, but nothing prepared for me for the onslaught of emotions that took over my mind and body as she spoke. Her parents, the aftermath, the abuse. By the time she was done, I was shredded.

This beautiful woman had endured so much and had chosen to share it with me. I kept up the façade of having it all together. It was better like that. If only she knew that I was just as broken, she probably would have made a different choice. Broken doesn't need broken.

Silence filled the room.

"Do you want me to take you home?" I asked because it was the right thing to say, not because it's what I truly wanted.

She paused. "Actually, no. I'd really like to stay. You make me feel good, Ashton. Unlike anyone ever has. And I feel safe. I trust you."

That was all I needed. Twisting my hand around the back of her neck, I gently pulled her toward me. "Let's take this slow, angel."

I showered her with kisses, my mouth tasting every last inch of her. We took our time, lazily touching and stroking each other, letting the need build slowly, organically. It wasn't how I typically did things but for some reason, it felt right. Like everything with Samantha, she seemed to feed parts of me I didn't know existed.

But the longer it went on, the more I wondered how much longer I could control myself. With my fingers inside her, she was getting closer and closer to the brink, and all I wanted to do was fall over it with her.

Finally, her lips pulled away from mine. Panting, she looked up at me. "Are we going to make out all night or can we get past third base?"

I raised a hand in surrender. "So, you're done with slow and gentle, angel?" I asked, surprised but grateful.

"I truly appreciate that, Ash, but…you make me feel like I never have and well… I want more of it."

She was blushing and it was just so damn cute.

"Then let's not wait another second. You have no idea how much I want to be inside you, Samantha. That tight little pussy of yours has been calling out to my cock for too long now." I answered, reaching over to my nightstand for the condoms I had put there.

"Uh…were you planning to have someone over?" She asked, looking at the large selection.

I winked at her as I slid one on. "Just you, angel."

I couldn't possibly wait another moment to be inside her. I climbed on top of her and lined myself up, leaning down to kiss her. She reached up, biting my lip, her eyes filled with lust. The shock and pain of her bite drove me wild. With one quick thrust I was inside her, stretching her, filling her with everything I had. The harder I thrust, the more she shook, again and again, until there was nothing left of each of us. We detonated and crashed together, lying spent and sated in each other's arms.

CASSIDY LONDON

Chapter 29

Australia

Samantha Jordan

"Good morning, beautiful girl."

His voice floated through my groggy mind, wrapping me in a warmth that I had never felt before.

"Mmm…" Was all I could respond as I stretched my arms over my head and slowly let the light into my eyes. As I did, those beautifully sculpted abs came into view. He placed a steaming mug of coffee down on the bedside table before adjusting the towel around his waist and sitting down on the bed.

"Angel…" He murmured, his voice as soft as the touch of his fingers in my hair.

Like everything with Ashton, this morning felt different. I was still acutely aware of the electricity simmering between us. After last night, I expected it to be gone, but as he looked into my eyes, emotions whirled up inside me and warmth spread through my body.

"Look at you, already showered. I should get up." I started, feeling uncomfortable. I had never wanted more from a guy the next morning. The fact that I did now made me feel vulnerable in a whole new way.

As I sat up, Ashton shifted but didn't move from the bed. Slipping his strong hands under my arms, he lifted me as if I weighed nothing but air and straddled me on his lap. With his arms wrapped around my back and his hands creeping up into my hair, I was instantly putty in his hands. He pulled my hair to one side and leaned in to my neck. Tilting my head to the side, he inhaled. His unshaven stubble tickled my skin, making me shudder. Then his lips ever so gently kissed the same spot. But gentle was only a precursor to the ravenous sucking and biting that came next.

"Fuck, I want to take you again and again, Samantha." Ashton growled between fervent kisses that were now bruising my lips.

"I'm all yours..." I drawled. Ashton made me feel so confident that I barely recognized the girl talking back to him.

"Arghh..." He growled, running his hands through his wet hair.

"It's killing me, Samantha, but I can't...believe me, the only thing I want to do right now is get back into bed with you, but something's come up..." He trailed off, looking pained.

"It's...uh...it's my mum, my foster mum. I'm still close with her and, uh...she called and asked if I could go home for a bit." Concern in his eyes was apparent, but something else, too. That distant look he had last night at dinner suddenly returned.

"What? I don't understand. Is something wrong?"

"Yes, she hasn't been feeling well and she has to go into the hospital for some tests. She's asked me to be with her. She left me a message last night. I've actually been up for a couple of hours trying to secure a flight." He held me tight as he nuzzled my neck.

HEATWAVE

"Okay, well, it's fine. Go figure it out. Be with your mom, of course." I was babbling and I knew it. It felt shitty to be sad when he obviously had to go. I didn't want him to think I was one of those needy girls, so I hugged him hard.

"Let me get out of your hair so you can get organized." I said, getting up and grabbing my things. "Anyway, I'm due at work this afternoon, so…"

His arms came around my waist and squeezed me one more time.

"You're amazing, angel. I'll text you while I'm gone."

Chapter 30

Australia

Ashton Chase

I decided to stop by the clinic before heading to the airport. Although we had said goodbye this morning and it was only for a short time, I wanted to see her face one more time before I left. And I kind of liked surprising her.

"Hello there! You here for Dr. Jordan again?" Smiled the receptionist as I walked in.

"I am, can you page her?" Just then, her phone rang and man ran in carrying a large dog in his arms.

"By the way, Mr. Chase, it's really great to see you again." She giggled as she picked up the phone and held her hand over the receiver.

"Also, I'm not supposed to send you in, but she's in the break room just down the hall, second door on the left. If you want to go...?" She trailed off as her attention turned to the man with the dog.

I nodded and began walking down the hall, but something struck me as odd with that girl. She had mentioned she thought I looked familiar the other day and now she was giggling like a teenager. Fuck...part of me wondered if she knew me, the real me. But then again, this was Australia. I might be easily recognized in England, but not here. Definitely not.

With every step I took, I felt a grin spread across my face at the thought of seeing Samantha again. She had showered and left in a hurry this morning while I was on a call with Dan. One more chance to hold her and kiss her before I left was exactly what I needed.

Finally, I found the staff room. Raised voices could be heard as I reached carefully for the doorknob.

"You thought you could run from me? You thought you could fuck me over like that? Think again, princess!"

Throwing open the door, I was shocked at what I saw.

A man leaned against the wall, his two hands on either side, clearly blocking someone smaller and weaker beneath him. He wasn't a big guy, but he was clearly intimidating whoever was on the other side of his anger.

Fucking bullies were everywhere.

"Excuse me!" I called out. "Who do you think you are …"?

He turned and that's when I saw it was her. Samantha. My Samantha. Blind rage took over my body and I was on him in a second. My fingers pushed up under his chin as my hand held fast against his windpipe.

"Who the fuck are you, asshole? Get your hands off her!" I growled, the words barely audible as they left my mouth.

I heard her cry out "Ash, don't, please!" But it was too late. I pulled back and in an instant, my fist connected with his face. His chin angled sideways as his head clipped back and he went down to the ground. I ran to her.

"Samantha, angel! What happened? Who is this guy? Did he touch you?" My questions were like a relentless firing squad, but they were the only thing that kept me from exploding.

She crumpled to the ground next to the man, making me question if they shared a history. But when I bent down and scooped her into my arms, she collapsed into my chest, her sobs now coming out harder and faster.

Looking over at the crumpled body on the floor, I wondered for a second if I had really hurt the guy. Not that I cared if I was honest, but I didn't need to draw attention to myself like that. I quickly checked his pulse and the gash on his face.

"He'll be bruised and sore but he's fine. He'll open his eyes in a minute. Shall we get out of here before he does?" I asked Sam, who was still trembling.

"Yes, but I have to work, Ash… thank you, though. That's Dave, he's…." she trailed off, sobs cutting her off once more.

"Come outside and tell me, angel. Work can wait a bit." I walked her out of the clinic and towards a bench just off to the side of the main entrance.

Samantha didn't answer, but she did allow me to lead her outside. We sat down and a few minutes passed as she tried to compose herself, wiping her eyes and taking deep breaths. I let her take her time. There was no rushing something like this.

Finally, she spoke.

"He's from back home, a New York colleague. Actually, he was the one who first told me about the opportunity to come here." She shuddered. It was obvious she was afraid of this guy.

"Did he ever…" Asking was hard, but I had to know. Even if it meant I'd want to go back in there and kill the bastard.

Chapter 31

Australia

Samantha Jordan

"No, he didn't, I mean, kind of, but I ..." Ashton's entire presence and now interrogation had taken me by surprise. I wasn't sure what he was asking, and if I was being honest, I wasn't sure that Dave had done anything wrong.

"Well, he…he makes me uncomfortable and the last few times, he's been more aggressive, but…"

"Did he put his hands on you? Fuck, Samantha, if he touched you…" The veins in Ashton's neck were pulsating hard, his face was red, and all the muscles in his body seemed tense.

"Calm down, Ash. It never got that far. I'm fine." I reassured him. In the back of mind, I wondered what would have happened if Ashton hadn't shown up when he did. I shuddered at the possibility.

We sat outside at the bench under a large tree. It was a secluded spot and one that I had sat at many times since I'd arrived in NSW. This trip to Australia had been so much more than I ever thought it would be. Somehow, in the midst of the craziness, I had met a man who made me feel worthy of something more than just a passing glance. And maybe, just maybe, there was a chance for me to experience something special.

I had discovered that Ashton was caring, protective, and gentle as much as he was cold, dominant, and determined. And yet, his dark side intrigued me as much as the light. Those sparkling blue eyes that could turn on a dime to midnight black enthralled me. And after what had just happened, the thought of him leaving for London left me feeling like I had been punched in the gut.

None of it made sense. Ashton was possessive and jealous, protective yet mysterious. He had lied to me about the very first thing you share with someone; your name. And yet, for the strangest reason, it didn't faze me. I knew that it should. My mind kept bringing me right back around to the fact that one lie leads to another and another. Yet when I looked at him, I could feel myself falling, falling harder and faster than ever before into a sea of warmth. *What was it about this man?*

"Yeah, so Dave was always a creep, he was always trying to get in my pants back in New York." I glanced up at Ash, who was literally sizzling with anger.

"Did you get a restraining order?" He growled out.

"Umm no. Listen, Ash, it's nice that you're all concerned, but I'm a woman, this is the kind of shit women deal with all the time."

I continued on, telling him how Dave wanted to come here together.

"Sam...you do realize that he wanted to be here with you and basically created a plan B so he could still get what he wanted? This is more than just a sleazy guy, he's a man who needs to be stopped."

Ash paused for just a second, just long enough to pull me into his arms. His eyes locked on mine and I felt entranced, possessed, and safe. His lips locked on to mine and kissed me slow and sweet but with that unmistakable passion that was pure Ashton.

"Listen, I came here because I needed to tell you that my London trip is confirmed. My mum needs me and I'm heading out tonight. It will only be for ten days, but I have to know that you'll be safe. Actually, I wanted to suggest it before, but now I know it's the right choice." He paused, his fingers lifting my chin and forcing me to look him in the eye.

"You're moving into the condo. I can't leave you like this. You're too vulnerable with Dave around. He'll probably be staying at the same flat and after today, there's no way I'll allow that."

He stated his case firmly. It was clear this wasn't up for discussion. It was a strange sensation, having someone care about you. I liked it, but it also felt a little stifling.

"Ash, please! Please don't make a big deal out of this! I'll be fine, I swear." His hands grabbed my shoulders as he stared deep into my eyes, lips inches from mine. And I could have sworn I heard a low rumbling deep in his chest.

"Samantha."

I paused. His stare never let go of mine.

"You will move into my condo until I return from London. And I'm letting my friend Bradley at the station know. It's his place and he will check in to make sure you're okay. I'm giving him your number. This is not a discussion."

I rolled my eyes. "Okay, sure. I appreciate all this, but it's just not necessary, Ashton."

The words were barely out of my mouth before his lips crashed down on to mine. My body ignited with a now familiar electricity. Unable to contain myself, I gasped at the sheer power of his touch. Images of the previous night flooded my mind, reducing me to putty in his hands.

Our moment didn't last long. The sound of my pager beeped once, then twice, and almost three times until I had no choice but to pull back from him, leaving my body empty, desperately missing his touch.

"I'm sorry…I have to go…when do you leave?" I asked again.

"Headed to the airport now, angel. I will call Bradley on the way. You make sure you stay at the condo. Understood?"

I nodded my head.

"Good girl. I'll text you when I land. Stay safe." He kissed the top of my head one more time and our fingers remained entwined as long as possible before we pulled away from each other.

I dried my tears and pulled myself together as I walked back into the clinic, turning only once to watch Ash drive off.

Ten days. I just had to avoid Dave for ten days.

When I walked back inside, my goal had been to suck it up and get on with my day. I definitely wasn't in the mood to chitchat. But, when Cynthia called my name and motioned for me to come over to her, I put on a fake smile and tried my best. I didn't need anyone asking me what was wrong.

"Hey girl, I don't mean to pry, but I just have to say…Oh My God, how is London's most eligible bachelor in person? Is he everything they say he is?"

It was like she was speaking another language. Granted, I was only half listening. "What? Sorry, Cynthia, I have no idea what you're talking about."

She stared at me, cocking her head to the side quizzically. "Oh…I…"

"I have to get back to work." I muttered, walking away. I really wasn't in the mood for small talk.

***

The rest of my shift was decent. Dave and Ann-Marie had left to get settled, and most likely to tend to his sore jaw. At least I didn't have to worry about running in to them.

As I gathered up my things and prepared to leave, I thought about sleeping in Ashton's bed and immersing myself in his scent. Staying there was actually going to be a good thing. I quickly texted Alli to let her know and started to make my way towards the front entrance.

"Dr. Jordan? Samantha!" called Cynthia from the desk.

I turned my head and waved but kept walking. But damn if she wasn't like a dog with a bone.

The clicking of her heels came running up behind me. "I didn't mean to upset you earlier! Really, I didn't. It's just that my mum is from London and she's always telling me about this guy. Apparently, he's super famous and always in the press! He's some billionaire finance guy to the elite. He hangs out with celebrities, even some royals."

She just didn't stop. Babbling a mile-a-minute while I stared, becoming more and more aggravated. I just didn't care about gossip and celebrity nonsense. But I also didn't want to be rude. Cynthia was a nice girl.

"Who? Who are you talking about?" I asked sweetly, hoping that giving her a few minutes would end this conversation sooner than later.

She laughed. "It's okay, I already told him he looked familiar to me. God, I can't believe you went out with William Ashton Chase. He's so fucking hot."

Chapter 32

London

Ashton Chase

Flying had always left me restless and anxious, but this time I was filled with something deeper. Concern, anger, and truthfully...a possessiveness that I had never felt before. I thought about Samantha the entire time. The Dave issue was weighing on me. Even though I had spoken to Bradley and he had promised to keep an eye on her, knowing I was too far away to help her was too much to bear.

And that was just how it felt to leave her.

Five days had passed since I had landed in the cold, damp winter of London, and I hadn't spoken to her. The first few times, I chalked it up to the time difference. But it didn't take long before I called her at work. Each time I did, I was told that either she wasn't there or she was in surgery. She wasn't returning my texts or even my calls. I'd even sent Bradley to see what was happening. And he reported back that he had seen her in the hospital, looking perfectly fine and smiling as she chatted with a co-worker. So, what was wrong?

Could it be that she was avoiding me? I wasn't sure. The last time I had seen her, everything had been fine. It had been fucking incredible, actually. Visions of Olivia and all the shit that she had put me through was churning in mind. Yet I knew Sam wasn't like that. We had shared something special.

I knew she wasn't thrilled that I had insisted she stay at the condo, but that couldn't be the reason. And although I had told her that Bradley would check on her, I hadn't mentioned that there was also a private security team charged with discretely keeping tabs on her. Had she noticed them? Was she angry about it? Why the hell was she not answering my calls?

The thing was, I didn't have a lot of time to dwell on it. Since the second the plane had touched down in London, it had been a whirlwind. My team had met me at the airport and we'd spent two straight days holed up in the office working on the Layton plans. And it was good that we did.

The party was brutal. Press were everywhere trying to get a good shot of me. Having been out of the country for a while only made me more high profile than before. I fucking hated this shit. It made me lose my focus.

Layton had grilled me at the cocktail, the dinner, and at the bar, and he had done it all in front of his closest friends and confidantes. And that had just been the public demonstration. Later in the evening after we had all been drinking, he ushered me into his private office and gave me the news.

"Chase, I like you." He said, clapping me on the back like we were old friends.

"As you know, I've been watching you for over a year now and tonight you proved that you don't falter under pressure."

I nodded solemnly.

"I'm going to give you my business. You'll get a quarter of my portfolio to start with. Triple it and you'll be in charge of all my investments by year end. Fuck it up and I'll make sure that little firefighting hobby of yours becomes your full-time gig once again." He winked.

Asshole.

"Yes, of course, I understand." I nodded again, hoping my disgust for him didn't override my excitement about getting the job.

"Just make sure you're in London when I need you. You know I prefer to meet in person."

"Absolutely, Mr. Layton." I nodded, silently knowing that I needed to get my ass back to Australia.

Our little private rendezvous was over as quickly as it had begun. But I had gotten what I came here for. Now it was time to get back to my girl.

The press were relentless. This was why I typically spent my time at home when I was in London. Every time I was out in public, it was a disaster. London's most eligible fucking bachelor was forever the headline. Made me want to throttle every last one of those reporters.

And this time was worse. I was worried about Samantha and I hated being photographed. I'd told my team from the start that I hadn't wanted to go to the party with a date, but they insisted it looked good. I knew they were right. If I showed up alone, the press were even worse. Any woman I stood next to would become their next target. So, there I was thinking about Samantha but with Clara on my arm.

Clara and I had history. She was one of the two girls that I always requested from Sylvia's agency. And she was the easiest to take out on the town. She was a part-time model and was comfortable in high profile settings. She was always my go-to when I needed a date. The only issue was that I usually fucked her after an event.

But this time things were different. I couldn't get Samantha off my mind. I wanted to hear her voice, touch her skin, and breathe in the scent that was nothing but uniquely her.

"So, Ash…" Clara whispered, lowering her head to the side as I exited Layton's office and took her arm in mine. "When do we get to ditch this party and head back to your flat?"

I took a deep breath. She was a nice girl and a great lay, but that's not how this evening was going to end. I led her out to the garden for some privacy and stopped when we were far enough that no one could hear us.

"So?" She asked again. "When do we…"

I cut her off. "Not tonight, Clara. Things have changed for me."

"Fuck, Ash…I knew something was off with you tonight!" She huffed. "You met someone in Australia, didn't you?" She asked, a little quieter this time.

I had to be honest with her, I didn't want any miscommunications. "Yes." I answered simply. Honesty didn't require an explanation.

Then Clara surprised me. "I always knew you'd find your girl, Ash. Just hope she appreciates what an incredible man she has." She said sweetly before reaching to kiss my cheek.

I wrapped an arm around her and held her close as I bent down to whisper in her ear. "Thank you, Clara. I really do appreciate it."

Suddenly a light blinded us both as the sound of the cameras filled our ears. Voices began yelling and calling out from everywhere. *Fuck!* Somehow the press were in here. Everywhere. Right in the damn bushes of Layton's private fucking garden.

"Sir! Excuse me! Mr. Chase!" They called. "You've been seen out with this lovely lady before. Are the two of you an item? Is it serious?"

The questions were coming faster than we could run. I grabbed Clara's hand and started pulling her away.

"Ow, Ash, please, my heel!" She cried. I looked down to see the heel of her shoe had broken off. "Fuck!" I muttered under my breath. I had no choice. If we didn't get out soon, they'd be all over us, spinning half-truths at best and out-right lies at most.

I knew it was a little caveman of me but it was also practical. So rather than think about it any further, I picked up Clara, threw her tiny frame over my shoulder, and ran back towards the house.

Chapter 33

Australia

Samantha Jordan

Reaching into the back of the fridge, I pulled out a bottle of white wine that Allison kept there. I was supposed to be at the condo, but everything there reminded me of him and our night together. I already felt like my insides were shattered, adding salt to my wounds was completely unnecessary.

Besides, nothing was going to calm my nerves like a glass or two of chardonnay. Adding ice to my already full glass, I walked back to the couch and sat down, sloshing the wine a little over the edge. I was being careless and messy and I didn't even have the energy to care.

It had been twenty-four hours since Cynthia had told me the truth. At first, I hadn't understood or even believed it, and I was still reeling from the shock. I needed to truly understand what I was dealing with. How things had gone from being naked and fucking blissful in Ashton's arms to feeling completely used and cast aside. Yet how unsurprising is it, that the second I let my guard down, I got slapped back in the face.

I should have listened to my gut. He'd run hot and cold the first time, then disappeared into thin air, only to come back and demand that I see him again. And I did. I got sucked in by that electric aura of his and disregarded the fact that he lied about his name. *His fucking name! Who does that?* Well, now I knew why. This is exactly why I didn't date. I'd been a magnet for fuck ups and sleaze balls since day one. Not much had changed since my early days with Gammy.

But on the other hand, it was hard to wrap my mind around why I was so upset. I really didn't know this guy from Adam. I really shouldn't have had any expectations of him. He was just a guy. A guy who delivered a baby koala and somehow wormed his way into my body and my emotions.

Shit. Even my own thoughts took me off guard. Maybe his physical appearance was clouding my typically solid judgement.

Solid judgement? Is that what you call it, Samantha? That damn voice was at it again.
More like shitty judgement.

I still hadn't looked him up. I was afraid that what I would find would be worse than my imagination. But I knew I couldn't continue without knowing. So, I chugged back a most ungraceful gulp of wine and quickly typed his name into the search bar on my phone.

William Ashton Chase.

Maybe I had been hoping Cynthia and her mom were wrong. Or maybe he had a doppelganger. Or maybe…Yeah, okay, none of that was the truth either. It had just taken me a bit of time to gather up the courage to check for myself.

Pictures flooded my screen and words seemed to zoom by at light speed.

London's wealthiest bachelor…financial guru to the elite…ex-firefighter…childhood house of horrors…

The information was coming at me so fast my brain could barely keep up. As fast as my fingers scrolled and clicked, my mind struggled to absorb it all, but I was barely breathing.

Who was this man? Certainly not a local firefighter as he had wanted me to believe. But why? If he really was the same as the guy in these pictures, why would he need to hide it? I looked a little closer. I would never fit with this type of lifestyle. Ashton wasn't just wealthy, he seemed to be billionaire status rich. His London flat looked like a mansion. He was pictured drinking and partying with Europe's A-list celebrities. He'd even attended the last royal wedding.

No wonder he had lied to me. What we had was never meant to be anything more than a fling. Bile began rising in my throat as fresh tears clouded my vision. But I kept going. Scrolling through endless pictures and articles until one in particular caught my eye. It was recent, just a day ago, at a party for someone named Fred Layton.

Is William Ashton Chase still London's most eligible bachelor or is he hiding a secret affair with model Clara Taylor?

The words made me choke on my wine but the pictures were worse…Ashton kissing the blond beauty, Ashton with his arms wrapped around her in a secluded garden, whispering in each other's ears. Ashton sprinting through the garden with her over his shoulder.

I began to shake, anger, embarrassment, and rage boiling up inside me, threatening to overflow. Clearly, I had meant nothing to him. He had made me believe that we had something worth trying for but clearly, I was nothing more than another notch on his belt. Maybe he'd finally thought better of it after our night together and decided to go back home where he belonged.

Allison would be back from work soon and I was in no state to talk. Ditching the wine, I moved to my bedroom where I could curl up in the blankets. The last thing I wanted was to have to pretend to be okay when I was anything but.

Chapter 34

Australia

Ashton Chase

There wasn't any more time to waste. I knew what I had to do. Get back to Australia and understand what the fuck was going on with my girl. She was still ignoring me, but at least I knew she was safe. The security team and Bradley had done their jobs well. They had stayed out of her way but kept a close watch. From what they had told me, she was going to work and hadn't been seen with Dave at all. However, she wasn't staying at the condo and that was really grating on my nerves.

I gave specific instructions to Bradley to ensure that Samantha would meet me. I trusted him to help make her comfortable enough to show up. Whatever the issue was, I was going to make sure we fixed it. But when he reported back that she was less than eager to see me and was only coming to give herself closure, I knew this was serious.

Everything between us had been perfect when I left. What could have happened?

Finally, seventy-two hours and jet lagged beyond belief, I walked into a café on the Sydney boardwalk and waited for her. Ten minutes later, she came storming into the café like a goddam tornado.

"First of all, you're a fucking liar. Either you start talking about London or I'm out of here." She stood with her arms crossed at her chest and fire burning in her eyes.

Fuck, that was her opening line? She stood in front of the little bistro table in a sundress that was too damn short to be decent. Those sinful tits with those pert little nipples poking through were such a damn tease. Chestnut brown hair flew in the breeze and a look of murder showed on her face. My heart ached to hold her and take away whatever was upsetting her. And it was all I could do not to grab her and fuck the anger right out of her on that very table.

"Samantha...please, angel, sit down." I said as I got up to pull out her chair, knowing by her reaction to me that I needed to tread carefully.

"Keep your damn English manners for the whores of London, Ash. I deserve better than being lied to."

A lone tear dropped from her eye and she raised a hand to wipe it as she stepped back.

"You're right. I did lie. I did, a lot. But let's get a drink first." I was still unsure about what I had lied about. I had admitted to the name issue, so what could this be about?

I needed to find the right words. But where did I start? I had everything planned when it came to her safety, but when it came to communication, I was starting to realize that I was a bumbling idiot.

"Start talking. Tell me about London."

"First tell me why you were avoiding my calls?" I growled back. "I was out of my mind with worry about you! Thinking about you having to work with that asshole, Dave."

"I don't owe you any information!" She glared at me. "I can take care of myself, I always have and always will. I don't need you riding in on a goddam white horse to save me. And if that's your idea of an explanation or an apology, you're really not the man I thought you were!"

She pulled away again and started speed walking down the ramp.

"Samantha!" I called after her. "What the hell?"

CASSIDY LONDON

Chapter 35

Australia

Samantha Jordan

His hand wrapped around the base of my neck and pulled me into him with one swift pull. A torrent of electricity went raging through me as our bodies connected. I could feel his hot breath on my lips as his own rested less than an inch away from mine. "You think you know who I am, Samantha?" He breathed into me, sending a new wave of adrenaline coursing through my veins. "You haven't got a clue." He continued, a snarl slowly spreading across his beautifully carved face.

He overpowered me in every sense, yet still, my emotions wouldn't allow me to back down. "But, Ash…what did you expect me to think?" I stammered shakily.

My words seemed to momentarily tame him as he released his hold on me and stepped back. Immediately, my body shuddered from the loss of his touch on my bare skin. I watched as larger than life Ashton Chase, the mysterious man who had more secrets than I could have ever imagined, stepped back, defeated. Those hands that had given me more pleasure than I had ever known were now running through his thick, dark hair with frustration.

I paused, uncertain of how to approach him. The air, heavy with words unsaid, blanketed the space between us. Seconds turned to minutes as despair welled up inside me. It was over. His silence told me as much.

"Last chance, Ashton." My voice cracked with emotion. "Tell me what happened in London."

Ashton sucked in a deep breath and held it, hands cradling his head in defeat. I didn't know if he was considering answering me or delaying the inevitable, but his silence was like a slow-moving poison to my heart.

Finally, I had no choice. Tears pricked the backs of my eyes as I turned to walk away. My feet felt like lead and my body was numb. Ashton Chase didn't feel anything for me. Maybe he never had. With each step, I could feel the resurgence of my old nemesis creeping up the back of my wounded soul. *You see, Samantha?* She sneered. *Nothing changes.* I felt myself breaking with every nasty word that my head threw at me.

I walked and walked, oblivious to the world around me. The sun was setting, people were in the street, even cars. My own personal hell was drowning me and I didn't even care. I was running now, desperately running, tripping, falling over my own feet. It was messy and frantic and I didn't care. I just needed to move. Faster and faster until I hit that cadence where I could just lose myself. My thighs began to burn and my breathing laboured as I drove myself faster and harder along the boardwalk. The endorphins kicked in and that familiar feeling of blissing out hit me hard. I let my eyes flutter in response and focused on it. Running was healing. Even when the pain was too overwhelming to bear.

A ramp approached and I exited the boardwalk. I kept my pace despite the feeling of the pavement hitting me. Instead of the soft rebound of the wooden planks, the harsh asphalt reverberated in my shins. But I didn't care. I needed this. I needed to block everything out and just run.

Despite the pain, something lingered. Was it hope? Desperation? I wasn't sure. But a little tingle appeared somewhere deep behind the remains of my heart; a little spark. A different voice.

HEATWAVE

He will come for you. I glanced behind me. Nothing.

My eyes fluttered again. I felt drugged, nauseous, and ...SLAM!

Nose down on the pavement, I froze, shocked, and unable to move for a second.

"Oh, my goodness!" Cried a woman's voice. I looked around, seeing grocery bags everywhere.

"I...I'm so sorry." I stammered. "I didn't see you." I jumped up, the feeling of sticky blood trickling down the side of my face. "Let me help..." I offered as I began to help her collect her things.

"Don't bother!" She yelled, shoving me away. "What the hell is wrong with you, girl? Who runs full speed with their eyes closed?"

She waved me away again and I began to move away from her. I truly wanted to help, but another confrontation, even a small one, with someone who clearly didn't want me, was just too much for me to handle.

I wiped the back of my hand across my brow trying to gather up the sweat and blood that had now mixed together. I must have looked demented, standing there with makeup mixed with blood, sweat, and tears trickling down my face. It was not my finest moment. I kept moving down the street before turning into the alleyway behind my apartment.

Even though it was the middle of the day, I knew Ashton would have told me to take the long way around the front and not to walk here. Well, fuck him. But yet, I felt him, somewhere in the back of my psyche, telling me to keep a look out and it pissed me off even more.

It wasn't more than a few steps before I felt his presence behind me. At first, I wondered if I had imagined it. *Wishful thinking?* But when the wind wafted his scent towards me, I knew. And as angry as I was, there was something else, too…hope.

I slowed my gait, pausing. He was quiet, but I knew it was him. His scent became stronger. Earthy, sensual, masculine. My heart lifted and my skin prickled with goosebumps in anticipation.

In an instant, he grabbed me, flipping me around as if I was nothing more than a feather. I felt my molars slam together and the cold, hard surface of the brick wall on my skin as he slammed me up against it. His fingers wrapped around my hair, pulling my neck back and forcing my chin up into his face. Those piercing eyes, no longer the cerulean blue from earlier but now a dangerous shade of midnight, seemed to penetrate my soul.

"Don't you ever run from me!" He breathed. His words barely registered in my brain before his lips crashed down and I felt myself melt into the ocean of pleasure that crashed over my body. But I wasn't going to let him in so quickly. I turned and tried to slip from his grip. But he was faster than I was. Strong hands grabbed my hips as he pressed his own to my ass, the hard length of him digging into my backside. It took everything I had not to arch my back and push into him. With one hand still under my chin and the other holding me fast between his hard body and the brick wall, I had nowhere to go. My mouth turned up of its own will as I craned my neck to see his face.

"Change your mind, William Ashton Chase? Feel like talking now?" I quipped, secretly thrilled beyond belief that he was actually here. Touching me. Breathing on me.

His eyes widened at my words but his hands never moved. Realization seemed to cross his face. "Shit...okay. I have a lot to answer to, I suppose."

"Just a bit." I spat back as I tried to detach myself from him.

He wasn't having any of it. "I'll tell you everything, angel, but the most important thing to know is that my feelings for you have been the truth since day one."

My eyes flooded at his words. I wanted so much to believe him but my heart felt like it had been trampled over. Words seemed useless, so instead I just nodded.

"Did you truly doubt me, angel?" His voice gravelled as his anger turned to desire. Hands reached back around me and roamed my body with a possessiveness that he had only hinted at before. This was a new Ashton, one that was authentic, raw, and made me quiver uncontrollably.

My skin came alive beneath his touch. Despite the aching in my heart, his touch was like a sledgehammer to my walls. I could feel them crumbling beneath the brute force that fisted my hair. His mouth crushed mine and that devious tongue of his continued to push, to intrude, and demand to be let in. I had no choice but to let him. I surrendered to the intrusion and relished in it. Ashton Chase was pure aggression and tenderness all in one and I wouldn't have had it any other way. I wanted whatever he would give me, even if it would destroy me in the end. Desire coursed through my veins, hardening my nipples into elongated tips that ached to be abused by those skillful fingers.

"You're so beautiful when you're angry with me, angel." He whispered as his teeth grazed the base of my neck, nipping my skin as he went.

My voice whispered, "You still owe me answers, Ashton." He brushed his fingers against my cheek, slowly wiping away blood stained with tears.

"I know I do. But we're also going to do this right, angel." He breathed into my neck, making all the hairs stand up on my neck. "Inside. Now." He said as he motioned toward the apartment door. I knew he wasn't giving me a choice. My body had already betrayed me, but I had to try and hold on to my heart a little longer.

"Ash, please. Let's just talk about this. Then we can go inside." I tried. "If we go in…" I trailed off, barely having the energy to finish my sentence. But I didn't need to. Ashton knew me better than anyone.

"Don't look at me like that. I know you're confused and I know I hurt you, but it wasn't willingly. I promise I'll tell you everything. But we will take care of this inside. You're bleeding, Samantha. Inside. Now!" He marched towards the front door of my building, pulling me along with him.

Fuck. I was supposed to be stronger than this. I was supposed to be in control. I wanted to be the one making the decisions, but truth be told, I was so goddam tired. Tired of fighting my emotions, tired of being alone, tired of second guessing everything he had ever said to me.

So, I let him lead me in. I would take whatever I could get because it didn't matter anymore, I was an addict when it came to him.

Chapter 34

Australia

Ashton Chase

There was no way in hell I was going to have this conversation in the back alleyway of her awful apartment. I still couldn't believe she was living here. She should have moved in to the condo by now. Damn, I had really fucked this up. I kicked myself for every stupid decision that I had made. I'd nearly lost her. I couldn't let that happen a second time around.

I should have just answered her at the café. Then she wouldn't be so mistrusting of my intentions. I had planned to, I just couldn't find the words. Then, before I knew it, she was walking away. By the time I had paid the bill and came out, she was gone. I panicked. I got angry and let my emotions get the better of me.

Now here we were, outside her door, and she was fumbling with the keys.

"Let me do it, angel." I whispered, gently covering her shaking hands with mine. She turned and looked up at me, her eyes still absent and glassy.

"Please." I asked again, willing myself to be gentle with her. I had learned that for as fiery as Samantha could be, it was all a mask. And I knew all too well that worked.

"Whatever." She shrugged, crossing her arms over her chest and stepping back from the door.

It opened and I reached for her hand as we walked inside. The pull to gather her up into my arms and shower her with kisses was overwhelming. But there would be time for that later. For once, I was going to try and speak with words. I owed her as much.

Once inside her flat, she let me clean up the blood on her face. Thankfully, she only had surface scratches, but it killed me that she was banged up because she had been running from me.

As we sat on the couch, I noticed how she perched on the edge, her body still tense. Creases in her forehead and around her eyes showed her true feelings even though her voice had now stilled. Void of emotion, she spoke.

"Ash...I appreciate that now you want to apologize, although I feel like I gave you that chance at the café and you just ignored me..." She trailed off.

"You're right." It was a simple answer but it was the truth.

She nodded quietly.

"So, let's talk." I began.

I watched as she took a deep breath and pulled herself up straighter. "I'm not the one who needs to talk here, Ashton. But I am the one who saw your picture splashed across British media with a fucking supermodel on your arm when you were supposed to be caring for your sick mother."

She spoke quietly, but her face was flushed with shame. "You told me you were going to London to see your mom who was having medical tests. Next thing I know, I find out that you're some billionaire who goes to charity events with supermodels!"

HEATWAVE

Samantha looked completely broken and she had every right to be. Her pain was real and I could feel it sucking me in, poisoning everything we had together.

"And I thought you were a freaking firefighter!" She was getting louder now.

"For fuck's sake, Ash, why did you lie to me? Am I not good enough for you?" She shook her head and brushed back some hair from her face. "I guess a broke American girl never had a chance at the real you anyway."

Her words broke me.

"You're right. I lied. And I'm not a firefighter. I mean I was, but that was a long time ago. But dammit, Samantha, I didn't lie about everything."

She paused and stared at me, new tears running down her face as she looked up.

"I didn't lie about how I feel about you. Never. Not once." I continued. "But you're right. I did go to London under a different pretense and that was wrong of me."

I watched as Sam exhaled slowly. This was good. She was listening.

"I'm sorry that I haven't been forthcoming with you about who I really am."

"Ash…what about everything I read online?"

"When it comes to my childhood or my business, most of it is true, angel. The press does love to elaborate on my personal life, though." I watched as she relaxed a little.

"Keep talking."

Taking a deep breath, I started at the beginning. My childhood. The fire.

"Sometimes I would see other kids get dropped off at school by their dads. I used to watch, mesmerized as they would hug each other goodbye. For many of them, you could really see their love. It was obvious in their smiles, in the pats on the back or in the ruffle of their hair. It seemed warm and magical to me." I sucked in more air. My lungs were already hurting.

"My home life was the opposite of all that. The only thing my dad liked more than his drink was inflicting what he considered to be discipline on my mother and I. Whether it was holding my head underwater or beating my mother within an inch of her life, he felt it was his duty to ensure we followed the rules. Except his rules were ever-changing. He tripped us up on purpose. The glean in his eye when he called my name has been burned into my soul forever."

There were so many questions in Samantha's eyes. But she only asked one. "What did your mother do?"

I felt a shiver crawl up my spine. "Nothing."

Samantha's hands reached out and covered mine with a squeeze. I hadn't realized they were shaking.

"He was exceptionally manic on the night of fire. Ripping the house apart as he searched for his cigarettes, throwing drunken slurs at both my mother and I. When he couldn't find them, he lunged for her. I could feel her bones cracking as his fist connected with them." I swallowed, my throat tight and parched.

"So, I ran to the shed to hide." I continued. "It didn't take long for him to come and find me."

"Boy! I know you're in there." He called, his voice floating through the air in a chant-like melody.

I sat on the floor of the shed, huddled with my face buried in my knees.

"Don't think you can hide, boy. I know it was you who hid my cigarettes from me. Get your arse out here and accept your punishment!" He bellowed.

This was the point where I usually conceded. I admitted to whatever wrongdoing he accused me of, even when it wasn't true. But not this time. This time, I made a different choice. I did nothing. I didn't speak, move, or even dare to breathe.

It enraged him like never before.

Minutes passed, my fingers in my ears as I tried to block out his voice. He could have just broken down the door to get to me. But that would have been too easy. He wanted to terrify me, torture me. Solidify his position as the almighty monster that he was.

"Seems you need a little help with your decision, boy."

I heard him approach the door and wait. Minutes ticked up as I strained my ears.

That's when I heard him strike the match. The sound of the friction was one I knew well. He did it every time he lit up a smoke. Only this time, he let that flame ignite the old wood shed.

"How long will you take to come out now, boy?" He mocked. "Will you brave the smoke and heat or are you ready to come running out into your daddy's arms?"

He was practically chuckling with his own perceived genius of the situation.

"Well…needless to say, it didn't take long for the old shed to go up in flames. Soon the choice to run out wasn't even possible. I remember the flames everywhere…the heat…Fortunately, the neighbours had heard the yelling and had called for help before he set the fire. The fire brigade arrived just in time…"

I watched as her face crumpled at the horrific details. She didn't interrupt me or look away. She let me talk and it felt…cathartic.

Finally, I told her about the last few years.

"I met Bradley in London. We worked together at the station for a few years and things were good. Until I was hit with the worst panic attack of my adult life. I couldn't function, couldn't do my job. I remember the smoke and how it filled my lungs. Everyone was screaming at me to get out, to run, but the flames were everywhere, and I could feel the heat through my suit. An overhead beam came crashing down and that was the last thing I remembered. I woke up in a hospital bed three days later with awful burns across one side of my body."

I spoke about Olivia and how her betrayal had ruined me. Shame filled me as the memories came flooding back. I released my grip from Samantha's hands and hung my head. Silence filled her tiny flat and it felt like hours passed before she spoke. Then suddenly her hand rested on my thigh. The warmth of her hand slowly brought me back to the moment.

"Keep going, Ash."

I explained how my accidental career had turned me into a local celebrity in London. Everything from the high-profile clients and how the press always hounded me. All my reasons for not giving her a chance to know the real me.

"I just didn't want to come out here and have people look at me differently again. I've been dealing with that my whole life, Samantha. When I was nothing, people pitied me, and now that I've made a something of myself, well, everyone wants a piece of it. I just wanted to be normal like everyone else."

"I get it." She nodded. "But things got really intense between us really fast. When you left, I thought it was the beginning of something that I've never had and thought I never would. So, when I learned the truth…it just seemed like everything I thought we had was just in my imagination."

She paused for a moment and looked down at our hands that were still entwined together. "And seeing you online with that woman, when I thought you were there for your mom…it made me wonder if I had been anything more than a casual fuck to you."

I cupped her chin with my fingers, tilting her head up to look at me. "Samantha, nothing about my feelings for you are casual."

Sam shifted in her seat, clearly still not trusting my words.

"I swear, my angel, I took her to that party because it was good for business to show up with a date. And I do have history with her, but we are nothing more than friends now." I continued on, explaining that night and everything that had happened at Layton's party.

"I will spend every waking moment making this up to you if you will let me."

She parted her lips as if to speak, but I didn't give her a chance. My mouth was on hers and I pushed my way in. Forcing her lips apart with my tongue, I swirled it around, reveling in the sweet taste of her. Samantha exhaled a little moan and my heart exploded at the sound, my cock already hard for her and straining against the confines of my jeans.

"I missed you so much, angel. Please forgive me?" I whispered between urgent kisses.

Chapter 35

Australia

Samantha Jordan

I hesitated. But he already had me. It was inevitable. Ashton Chase had always had me. And now, as his hand cupped my chin and his lips covered mine, I knew that despite what had happened, I was still willing to give in. My body consistently betrayed me whenever I was around him. I responded so eagerly to his touch and practically begged for more, but my mind still hesitated. Maybe I could forgive him, but could I trust him? I wasn't sure I could survive something like this again.

"Ash." I whispered between his kisses.

"Yes, my angel." He answered as his strong arms wrapped around me as we leaned back into the couch. He pulled me over him, using my body to blanket his.

He pulled my legs apart, forcing me to straddle his lap, and nuzzled his face in my chest. My breasts felt heavy and my nipples ached. I longed for him to take me hard and fast and make all the feelings in my head disappear. My body responded to him shamelessly. With my dress pushed up around my waist and my bare legs rubbing against the rough material of his jeans, it was hard to stay focused. But there was more I needed to say.

With my palms on his chest, I pushed back.

"Ashton." I began. "It's always like this between us. We have insane chemistry, but we suck at communication. Maybe we need to establish our limits. Maybe all we have is great sex. Maybe we either accept that for what it is and not have any more expectations or we don't do this…I'm just not sure I can handle my feelings for you."

I could feel the lump in my throat quickly rising. I turned my head and blinked back tears. *Why was this so damn difficult?*

"Samantha. We have done this all wrong since day one. But not anymore. This is it for me. You are it for me. From the very first moment I saw you outside the clinic, to every time I hear your voice, and see you smile, I know it. But I was scared at first. Scared of losing myself, of being judged, and mostly, I didn't think I could give you what you deserved."

My chest felt tight and the pain inside my ribcage ached with an intensity I had never felt before. As if he could feel it too, Ashton's hand reached forward and rested between my breasts.

"But I know better now. I just didn't listen to my heart the first time. But now I know. I know that I need you more than air. I will do anything to prove to you that I'm the man you need."

His words brought a smile to my lips.

"I'm absolutely prepared to beat the shit out of Dave for you, too. I never want you around that guy again. Still can't believe I left you with him after what he did." He growled.

That made me chuckle. "He couldn't do much when there was a private security team watching my every move."

He was incredulous. "You knew?"

"It wasn't hard to notice, Ash."

"Fuck it, I will spend all my time making it up to you. I promise. Give me a chance to prove myself."

His eyes were begging me and it went straight to that tiny little flicker of hope that remained, igniting it and allowing me to dive back in to everything that was Ashton Chase.

I smiled. "Don't fuck up this time."

"Never again." He growled, his eyes darkening as he pulled me into his embrace.

Those simple words made my body tingle, that familiar feeling soaring through me like a firecracker exploding. Wetness pooled in my panties, my nipples burned to be touched, and the ache between my legs intensified. My body wanted him as much as my heart did.

Sensing what I needed, he wrapped his hands around my ass and stood up, marching into the bedroom. His fingers squeezed the soft flesh of my ass in a way that I knew would leave marks I would see for days.

Kicking the door closed, he made his way to the bed, still devouring my mouth and sucking on my already swollen bottom lip.

"Angel, tonight we're going to do this differently. You know that I love our nasty, angry fucking as much as you do, but you also need to know how much I care about you. Tonight, I want to worship you for the beautiful, strong, passionate woman that you are. I want to share my heart with you."

He fluttered gentle kisses down my neck and across my collarbone as he spoke. The lightness of his touch made me squirm.

With feather light fingers, he slowly slid the straps of my dress down my shoulders, baring my skin. The cold air nipped at my skin, raising goosebumps.

"So beautiful." He murmured.

I tried to wiggle out as he pulled it down to expose my breasts, but he stopped me.

"Don't do anything. Stay still, don't move. I need to worship you."

His words made me giggle as I turned my head. He pulled the dress down, exposing my nakedness.

"No fucking bra." He murmured to himself as he shook his head. "Fuck, Samantha, when you walked into the café and I saw you, it didn't matter that I knew you were angry with me, my cock wanted you so bad it hurt. Such a little tease." He continued making me giggle.

"Lift your hips." I complied, my dress sliding down my legs as he pulled on it, letting it slide to the floor. Naked except for my panties, I felt exposed but safe.

"Why don't you join me." I asked as I lifted the edge of his t-shirt, desperate to see those rock-hard abs that I knew were hiding.

"Not yet, sweetheart, this one is all about you. I love fucking you, Samantha, but tonight, tonight I want to make love to you." His lips were inches from mine as he spoke, his hands trailing down my naked flesh, but it was his words that made me shiver with emotion.

HEATWAVE

Tears once again pricked my eyes as I finally realized what I felt for him. I was in love with Ashton Chase and had been this entire time.

I kissed him back as his hand slipped between my legs and gently pulled aside my panties. "So wet, my angel. So wet for me." His fingers lazily strummed through the slick folds of flesh, making me pant with anticipation. "I'm going to make you wait for it tonight, my love. I want to hear you beg for it."

Ashton continued to kiss every inch of my body. "I need to feel every inch of you between my lips tonight." As his lips descended from my collarbone to in between my breasts, his fingers gently circled around my nipples without ever touching them. He seemed intent on turning me into a squirming mess of vibrating nerve endings. I wanted his hands everywhere but he was deliberate in his touch, caressing everywhere but the areas that screamed his name.

Licking, kissing, and the occasional nip of his teeth was all I got; my arms, the delicate skin on my stomach, around the underside of my breasts.

"I love your ribs, let me count them." He whispered, half chuckling as he gently kissed each one, his lips leaving a trail of wetness across my ribcage and between my breasts. I could feel my breath constricting from the sensations.

"Please, Ash, you're killing me." I managed, my breathing erratic from need.
"No, angel, just taking my time and enjoying every part of you." He answered as he raised up one leg, then the other, placing both over his shoulders. Kneeling between my legs, he lowered his mouth and gently blew air across my heated center.

"You have the most beautiful pussy, Samantha…look at her…" His fingers trailed across my slick folds, gently pulling them apart. "She's calling to my cock... so pink, soft, and so wet. Fuck angel, I can't wait to bury myself inside you."

Ash bent down again, his face just inches from my pussy, and inhaled. "Damn, you smell so sweet. It's addictive." His tongue flattened out as he licked me up and down, making me cry out in need.

"Fuck, Ash, please!"

He knew what I wanted, what my body needed, but the glint in his eye told me I wasn't getting it anytime soon. Leaning over, he kissed me, the tart taste of my own arousal on his tongue. I could feel myself shaking.

"Turn over, angel." He breathed as he flipped me over, gently guiding my knees up under me, my head resting on the blankets. His mouth circled around my neck, continually showering kisses down my spine. The cool bite of the air raised up goosebumps on my skin as his wet lips passed by. I was still incredulous at how he made me feel. I had never felt so free and so desired as I did with Ash. He seemed to know exactly what I needed at just the right time.

"How did I get so lucky that the most beautiful woman in the world not only gave me one chance, but has granted me two?" His hands cupped and massaged my ass as he spoke.

I gave him a wink from over my shoulder. "Just remember, two chances are your limit, mister."

He looked at me without blinking. "I'll never forget, I promise." I could feel his sincerity seeping in to all the cracks in my armor.

"And angel, don't think I forgot about your past, either. I want to love and worship your body in ways that will erase all those awful memories. No one will ever hurt you again, I will make sure of it."

My heart exploded right then and there. There were no words good enough to acknowledge his promise. Nothing but feelings that overpowered every cell in my body. He leaned in and kissed me softly, so gently that it brought fresh tears to my eyes. If this was what it felt like to love, I never wanted to feel anything but.

His lips left mine as his fingers gently trailed down the crack of my ass, spreading my knees wider, and down to my aching wetness between my legs. He circled twice, ever so slightly brushing against my clit, making me shudder before pushing a finger inside me and curling it around ever so gently before sliding it back out again. Like a cat in heat, my head raised and my back arched as I pushed up on to my hands and knees.

"My good girl, you want more?" He asked, continuing to tease my swollen flesh gently as he moved behind me and between my legs. I tried to speak but only hissed in desperation, clawing at the blankets.

As my back arched further, his finger found its way back to my ass.

"You're so beautiful, Samantha. I want every part of you." He circled my opening, spreading the slick evidence of my arousal around and around in the most forbidden of places. "Relax, angel, I won't hurt you."

I exhaled. "I know…I like it, it feels good."

I swear I heard him smile. "That's my girl."

He didn't stop, not even as his other hand found its way to my clit. Moving his hands in perfect harmony, he distracted me as he gently pushed through that sensitive ring of muscle. For a split second, I froze. The intrusion was not uncomfortable, but a strange and different sensation that made me pause for a moment.

"Samantha, you okay? Angel?" He asked, concern evident in his voice.

I exhaled again and smiled. "Fucking perfect." My answer made him chuckle.

"Well, we're only just getting started, angel…" He answered before sliding down between my legs, once again licking and nipping at my most sensitive parts. He continued on, matching the rhythm of his tongue on my pussy with his finger in my ass. He alternated between circling and sucking on my clit and tongue fucking me. Sensations were overwhelming. The softness of his tongue, his five o'clock shadow rubbing against my inner thighs, the back-door intrusion, all worked together, enticing and beckoning me toward that ultimate crescendo.

"Come for me, angel, come all over my face." He said. "I want to taste you, drink you in."

Those last words were all I needed to let go. The feeling came fast and hard, sparking up from the depths of my body as if ignited by some unknown accelerant. I heard myself scream as it burst forth, a crescendo unlike I had ever experienced.

The air stilled as I came down from the high. I lay there like a rag doll as Ashton held me in his arms.

"So perfect." I mumbled as he rolled me over on to my back.

"You're perfect, angel." He answered. "But I'm not done with you yet. I need to be inside you."

I hadn't even noticed, but somehow Ashton had shed his clothes. His golden, muscular body now hovered over mine, making me feel small beneath him. His hands began exploring my body again, while that incredible mouth of his nuzzled into my neck, instantly making me wet once more.

"I need you, angel." His voice was husky with desire.

"I'm ready for you, Ash." I answered, eager to give him whatever he wanted.

He didn't wait a second longer. With one swift movement, he lifted himself up, spread my legs, lined himself up at my entrance, and impaled himself inside me. I felt my body stretch and fill to accommodate him. Waiting a moment for me to adjust, he brushed his lips against mine, the gentle touch of his skin making me tremble.

My head was spinning and my body tingled with anticipation. "You feel so good, Ash…"

That was all it took. We instantly found our rhythm like it was a melody we had known all our lives. Back and forth, our bodies perfectly molded together in harmony. I felt every muscle twitch in his body as I ran my hands down his back. The strength and power of his movements were magnetic. It didn't take long before the nerve endings in my body all began firing at the same time and beckoning me towards the light.

"Open your eyes, angel. I need to see you."

My eyes fluttered open as his words continued to fill my ears.

"I can feel your pussy sucking my cock in. You're so fucking tight, angel. I want to feel you come all over my cock."

His words were like a drug to my body, instantly making me comply. I stared up into those deep blue eyes and felt myself being sucked in deeper. I watched the veins in his neck pulsate as the tightly wound coil inside me sprung forward, first like a warning bell, then like an all-out siren. As we both exploded into an abyss of pleasure, certainty hit me like a tidal wave. This man was irrevocably branded into my soul.

Chapter 36

Australia

Ashton Chase

My alarm went off far too early the next morning. The sun was just peeking through the curtains. She was still breathing softly, wrapped up in my arms. I wanted to kiss her, wake her, see every moment of those beautiful, brown eyes opening. But I didn't dare stir. The feeling of her naked body against mine was too good.

Last night had been incredible. I could only hope she would feel the same way I did.
As the sunlight became stronger, I felt her breathing change and she stirred.

"Angel?" I whispered. Her neck craned and I released my hold on her so that she could turn around to face me.

"Morning, Ash…" Her sleepy voice whispered as she smiled. *Oh, that smile.* I wanted to wake up to that smile every day.

She giggled. "Last night was so awesome."

Her nipples grazed against my bare chest as she rolled over, electrifying my pulse. Instinctively, my fingers reached for them, rolling them beneath my fingers and teasing them to a point.

"Fuck, you drive me crazy, Samantha. I'm so hard for you, look what you do to me." I breathed as my cock pushed up against her thigh, searching desperately for her heated center.

"I need you, angel." I brushed hair from her face and searched her eyes.

"Well, I'm a little sore from last night, but looks like you're getting me all hot and bothered again." She giggled.

"Fuck yes…" I hissed. "Last night I was all soft and gentle but I can't promise that this morning, my angel."

"You know what…" she paused. "I kind of like these different sides to you. Why don't you show me what you want now?"

Her words were barely out of her mouth and my fingers, which had been gently brushing back and forth against her nipples, gave a hard squeeze. My balls tightened painfully as I twisted and watched the lazy smile instantly change into pain and shock on her face.

Climbing on top of her, I used my knee to spread her legs, feeling her slickness on my skin as our bodies connected. My lips met hers and I forced my tongue inside, ruthlessly taking what I wanted, what I needed from her. She was everything, this woman. She was my addiction and I needed to tell her.

I pulled back and watched her half open eyes flutter. "Samantha…my angel…"

She smiled again.

"You are everything I ever wanted. I want to wake up like this every day, with you in my arms. Making you come undone for me. Again, and again until you never doubt that this is forever. I love you, Samantha Jordan, and I will spend the rest of my life showing you."

My angel gasped, her hands flying to her mouth as tears immediately filled her eyes. "Oh Ash, I love you, too!"

I didn't need anything more. I leaned in and kissed her with everything I had as we whispered those precious words over and over again.

"On all fours for me, angel." I said gruffly, my voice heavy with both desire and emotion. "I need to see that beautiful ass of yours." She complied, spreading her knees wide, her head hanging low, her beautiful hair splayed out across the pillow.

"This is what I want, Sam. Every fucking morning, I want you naked and wet for me." I grabbed a fistful of her hair and whispered in her ear. "You know why, precious? Because you're mine. Now, today, tomorrow, and forever. I love you. You are MINE."

I impaled myself in her heat, giving her only a moment to adjust before rutting against her harder and faster than I had the night before. My hand slipped between her legs and found her hard, swollen nub, rolling it between my fingers as I thrust into her. Her pussy clenched and pulsated around my cock. When I felt her start to shake I let go, spurting my seed inside her, filling her up and claiming her once and for all, as my one and only.

CASSIDY LONDON

Epilogue

San Francisco

Adriana and Tristano's Wedding

Adriana was a beautiful bride. Of course, we knew she would be. Ava and I held each other's hands as we stood at the altar and watched our friend walk down the aisle. I tried to swallow back the lump in my throat that grew with every note in the music.

"Hold it together, Sam!" Whispered Ava as she squeezed my hand. "If you can't get through Adri's wedding, you'll for sure be blubbering all through your own!"

I had to laugh. She was right.

Looking over at Ashton sitting in the front row, I smiled. He winked at me, but I noticed his eyes were a little glassy, too. Our wedding wasn't for another year, but that was only because he insisted on making a big deal out of it. I would have been perfectly fine with a small ceremony of just our close friends. But he wanted all of the UK to know that London's most eligible bachelor was off the market. He'd rented a castle in the countryside for the reception and had already sent out invites to the press. For a guy who used to hate them, he sure had changed.

As Adri and Tris recited their vows, I thought of my own. Mine would be simple. I only needed to speak my truth. For so long I had been lost, damaged, stuck in the past. But Ashton had changed all that for me. He had given me back my life.

Because of him, I finally learned that living meant being touched by a love so deep, it heals all your broken pieces. That's what William Ashton Chase had done for me. He'd healed all my broken pieces.

Just as the priest said his final words to Adri and Tristano, I looked over at Ashton one more time. He smiled and mouthed, "I love you, Samantha Jordan."

The End

Please take a moment to review this book so that others can enjoy it too!

Dear Reader,

Thank you so much for picking up this book, it truly means the world to me. If you enjoyed this series, I know that you will love the stand-alone INKED LOVE! The MC's of Inked make a cameo appearance in Layover (International Love 2) so you might already be familiar with JM and Lexi.

A small excerpt of INKED LOVE is included for you in the next few pages.

Happy Reading!

Cassidy xo

CASSIDY LONDON

INKED LOVE

An Enemies to Lovers Romance

Prologue

A delicious aroma came flooding through my nostrils and registered hard into my brain. My mind and palate reeled with anticipation, hoping to catch a glimpse of what was producing such a mouthwatering scent. However, it seemed that I would not be given the opportunity...

She kept urging me on, faster and faster, until my legs were barely able to keep up and the burn was cramping my calves. We finally turned the corner onto yet another narrow cobblestone street, when the sound of laughter and dishes breaking, filled my ears. Despite this, my focus remained steadfast as I continued skipping over the stones, each more uneven than the next.

Inhaling deeply for the second time that evening, I took in the most enticing scent. Unmistakably, I recognized it as *poutine*; that infamous gravy and fries dish renowned here in the Province of Québec. It was greasy, gooey and bad for you in all the best ways. Or so, I assumed anyway from what my friends had told me.

Closing my eyes for a moment, I focused on another forbidden scent. Cigarette smoke and beer. I loved the way it seemed to blanket the city's thick summer heat. There was something sublimely perfect about that moment. And despite it lasting only a few seconds, it would remain etched in my mind, forever.

My mother rushed along even faster than before, her heels clicking repeatedly along the uneven stones. She tugged at my hand impatiently as I slowed down to gaze at the hordes of loud, boisterous patrons on a nearby terrace. From the corner of my eye, I caught my mother's nose wrinkle in disgust at the sight of cheese curds sprinkled atop of their food. People were laughing and calling out "bon appétit!", as they dug into these seductive dishes. They seemed happy and relaxed in a way that I had never experienced or seen in my immediate surroundings. It was amazing that we were only six hours from home, and yet the people of Montreal, seemed to be living in a different universe.

"Alexis stop ogling; it's such a classless behavior." My mother scolded loudly as if her judgmental behavior was perfectly acceptable. As usual, my father was strides ahead, pretending he wasn't even with us. Talking on the phone as always; he was immersed in a world of cases, depositions and problems that seemed far more important than us. My older brother Logan was trailing even further behind, but no one seemed to notice or care about him. Just me. How typical.

I tried to keep up with my mother's pace but it was next to impossible. She was on a strict schedule, as always. Aiming to be exactly down to the minute, and if possible-- even the second. I, on the other hand, would have been content to wander the streets leisurely and take in all the fascinating sights and sounds. Looking up at her, I smiled. Despite my annoyance at her constant lecturing, her beauty captivated me. I had always been told that I was a carbon copy of her. And I couldn't deny that we both had the same thick, bouncy white blonde hair and crystal blue eyes. Our skin was a light caramel color from the summer sun. But our differences ended there. Where she sported a hard-stern stare, I offered a distant dreamy innocence.

That look was not for anything. I had learned long ago, how to keep her happy. Agree, placate, smile, and repeat. It was a cycle that was so familiar to me it was almost natural. Except that it wasn't. And somewhere, somewhere far off and deep within in my being, I knew it.

We continued around that last corner and ran straight into a mass of people dancing, singing and clapping in tune to a street band. Needless to say, my mother's mood went from bad to worse. What she perceived as such low-class behavior, nearly gave her a coronary. She just kept muttering under her breath about the loud music and the scandalously clad young women, dancing in the streets. Like oil to her water, I was mesmerized. Hypnotized, by the freedom that they joyously displayed. They seemed to dance without a care in the world, and in that moment, I wanted to be one of them.

Glancing behind me, I saw that Logan was looking equally entranced, but perhaps for a different reason. We caught each other's eyes and he smirked as I rolled my eyes back at him. We weren't really all that close, Logan and I. However, in times of allegiance against the uptight, rigid, rules of the roost-- we were always in each other's corner.

Finally, we had reached our destination and caught up to my father. We slipped dutifully in the lineup behind the other guests. It seemed that everyone had arrived at the same time which forced us to halt and wait for our turn to enter. My mother brushed the creases in my dress and fussed with my hair aggressively. Her attempt to fix the errant strands of hair that had been messed up during our speed walking, only made it worse. She made my fifteen-year-old self, feel like I was five in an instant.

Standing there and trying to ignore her while she fussed, I shifted my focus to a nearby door. A door that was dark, sinister and yet so very intriguing. It had an aura that made shivers go up my spine as I silently wondered what was happening on the other side. No signs or markings had given me a clue.

As if the universe was answering my thoughts, the mysterious door opened, and a man appeared. He leaned against the arched door frame and lit up a cigarette. It was impossible not to stare at him despite knowing that every second that I did, would get me into more trouble than it was worth.

His jeans hugged his lower body in a way that made me stare at places that I hadn't before. His t shirt clung to the rippled form beneath the thin white cotton. His arms and neck were lined in an array of tattoos that left almost no natural skin showing at all. He had a five o'clock shadow and a black tuque that hung off the back of his head, despite the summer heat.

My erratic, heavy breathing soon caught my mother's attention. She leaned in to my ear tactfully, and whispered, "Stop staring Alexis. Despite him being an unsavory character, it's still rude." Her voice stung me with a sickly sweetness.

HEATWAVE

Unfortunately, my mother hadn't been subtle enough though. In fact, she may have even caused him to notice me. Or... maybe not. In any case, we locked eyes as he flicked his cigarette in our direction and lifted his chin towards me like he approved of what he saw. He held my gaze long enough that my heart began to pump faster in my chest and my breathing faltered in rhythm. I could feel the prickly heat of embarrassment and curiosity dancing its way across my chest. Looking away was impossible. He held me, captive and entranced. He was definitely way older than I was, but he looked at me not as the little girl my parents saw, but as the woman I desperately wanted to be. It couldn't have been more than a few seconds but it felt like an eternity before he threw his cigarette on the ground and winked at me as he ground it out with his foot.

Logan brushed past me and whispered in a sing-song voice, purposely loud enough for my mother to hear, "Ooohh... looks like Lexi's got a thing for older bad- boys, eh?"

Appalled, my mother grabbed my face below my chin and yanked it to get my attention. "Don't you even think of it young lady!" She scolded. Shaken out of that most blissful moment, I sighed turning to her. This was the story of my life. Being reprimanded for something before I'd had the chance to even consider it.

"If you ever come home with tattoos-- or with a boy who looks like that, you'd better just not come home at all!" She continued on, rambling about how respectable young women should behave. Once again, I plastered a zombie-like smile on my face and zoned out.

CASSIDY LONDON

Chapter 1

It was right smack in the middle of my twenty-fifth birthday party in front of all our friends and family, when Jason my boyfriend of four years, surprisingly professed his undying love for me.

"Alexis Reynolds, I love you and want nothing more than to spend the rest of my life with you…you and your beautiful family." Jason eyes pulled away from mine and looked out into the crowd.

My gaze followed his as I watched him lock in on my father. They both nodded a seemingly silent agreement between them. Turning back to me; those blue eyes once again sparkling in my direction, he pressed on. "So…will you marry me Alexis?" he asked.

Looking down into those clear blue pools, I smiled nervously. The man that had swept me off my feet in college and had been an overnight hit with my insanely hard to please family, was now down on one knee, asking for my hand in marriage. I had waited for this moment forever. It seemed we all had.

I buried the emotions that were simmering under the surface and tried to focus on what was being presented before me. Unfortunately for me, this was not the private, romantic moment that I had envisioned. No, this was actually the complete opposite. We were standing in the middle of a lavish room, in one of Toronto's best restaurants; with everyone we knew staring eagerly, anticipating the only acceptable answer.

I took a deep breath and shifted my focus to the black velvet box Jason held open. It was a beacon begging for attention, but blinding me like a solar eclipse as it flecked in the lights. *Oh God.* I could never wear that. It looked like it belonged in a museum. It was garish and embarrassing, just like Jason. He was loud, extravagant and dead set on being the center of attention at all times. His words and actions often made me cringe. *Maybe that's why he liked me?* After all, my dad had always said that being "behind the scenes" was more my strength.
Despite our differences, I couldn't deny that he was definitely handsome in his tux tonight. His cerulean blues were sparkling with joy as he looked up at me. His perfectly straight smile and smart clean haircut only served to accentuate that "type A" personality that I knew so well.

Jason had been suave, charming and determined to excel in everything-- when we first met. A competitive swimmer all throughout high school and college; he had that typical athletic build. He was the confidence to my shyness, the life of the party to my wallflower. Jason was the guy that everyone wanted to be around, and he had chosen me. The clean-cut, preppy young lawyer, that seemed to have jumped off the pages of a Ralph Lauren ad. Jason oozed charm. In public, he always had his arm around me, holding me close. Showing me off like a prize pony, making sure that everyone knew he was dating the daughter of the most prominent lawyer in the city.
The crowd had gathered around us and I could hear the cries of, "Say yes Lex! Say yes!"

I smiled through the uneasiness that was building in the pit of my stomach. I hated being the center of attention. I knew I needed to stop stalling and give them what they wanted. Pulling myself up straight, I smiled and nodded quickly. Jason wasted no time pulling me into his embrace and dipping me backwards. And of course, making a spectacle out of every passing moment once again. The crowd cheered.

His lips came down on mine with a heaviness that seemed rehearsed. I had always hoped that there would be stars, rainbows and glitter falling from the sky when the love-of-my-life asked me to marry him. I expected a surreal moment, where time stood still and everything slowed down to a quiet hum like you see in the movies. As always though, my expectations were off the charts. It made for a consistently disappointing life. But really, I had no reason to complain. My life was exactly as it was meant to be. Dictated and predictable.

So how did I get here exactly? Well, it's a simple but not so simple story.
First, let's start with tonight. It was just supposed to be a birthday party. But nothing was simple with Jason. He had planned a lavish celebration for me at the trendy French-Canadian restaurant "Sassafraz", in the heart of Yorkville. It was everything a girl could want. *Except for this girl.*
Everyone we knew was here. Our own private party surrounded by a living wall of vegetation lining the dining room. It was the type of event that would definitely make tomorrow's social news.

Despite my reluctance, it certainly wasn't anything that I wasn't used to though. It was common for our family to be the center of attention. My father was a founding partner at Reynolds & Cunningham. He had been a top dog at Finnegan & Martineau for decades and finally had fulfilled his life-long dream of opening his own firm. Everyone said he would fail, but of course my dad, being the shark that he was, had proved them all wrong. His specialty was litigation and he was the best in the business. Needless to say, arguing with my father was an exercise in futility. My entire life, my dad had been in the limelight and by default-- so had our family. This night, my twenty-fifth birthday, wasn't any different.

There was a time when I had wanted to follow in my dad's footsteps and be a bad-ass lawyer just like him. I envisioned myself helping people and making a difference. Unfortunately for me, my dad had wanted my brother Logan to pursue a career in law, but not his daughter. Logan however, had other plans.

Right after high school, my older brother had announced that he would not be going to college. Instead he was going to backpack his way across the country and just take things as they came. Our parents were devastated but no one more so than my dad. Logan had totally blindsided them and they never got over it. From then on, I tried to make up for Logan's choices by working extremely hard in school, but it was never enough. It didn't matter that I graduated as valedictorian, with honors, or that I won scholarships to the top law schools in the country. They had wanted-- Logan. But Logan didn't give a shit. He spent the next few years smoking pot and snowboarding in Whistler, British Columbia. He never came back.

Maybe he had the right idea all along.

I remember very clearly the day my parents suggested I switch from pursuing law itself, to settling for a career as a paralegal. My boyfriend Jason was being sought-after left, right and center by all the top firms. He was currently considering all of them, and narrowing down his options.
It was over our ritualistic afternoon tea, that my mother had quietly suggested to me that there was a way for us all to get what we wanted. Dad needed a partner at his new firm, and Jason was the right fit. Jason would be able to rise to partner sooner rather than later in a smaller firm. And with the two of them at the helm, I could take advantage of the easy life. There was no need to slave away through law school when I could ensure I would be taken care of.

HEATWAVE

"It is the right thing to do" she said to me. "Give this opportunity to Jason and your father." The men were better suited to that line of work anyway. Plus, it would ensure that Jason stayed in Toronto. *I didn't want to risk him leaving the city or worse-- the province, right?*

It wasn't long after that I saw the two of them smiling and patting each other on the back like old friends. Despite it feeling like a knife had been stabbed through my heart, I believed or perhaps was conditioned to believe, that I had made the right decision.

From that day forward, my dad gave Jason everything he had ever wanted. A corner office, with all the perks, leads in all the top cases, and a showering of praise at all times. Jason's ego grew day by day and soon, I was more than happy to find reasons to stay away from the office.

Why work so hard when Jason was already taking care of everything? Besides, Jason had made it clear that he wanted a wife and eventually a mother holding down the fort at home. I definitely wouldn't need a law degree for that. You would think that I'd be crushed, right? Wrong.

It was a safe and comfortable place, following directions. Voicing opinions that rivalled those of my family had only ever resulted in disaster. Love was conditional and for a long time, I was more than willing to pay the price.

Nothing lasts forever though.

CASSIDY LONDON

Praise for INKED LOVE:

"The sexual tension between Lexi and JM was palpable. This book is a shining star! So well written."

-5 STAR Amazon Review

Want to read more of Inked Love?
Grab an eBook or paperback copy from your favorite book store today!

Join Cassidy's Reader Group on Facebook:

Cassidy's Confidantes

http://bit.ly/CassidysConfidantes

CASSIDY LONDON

Acknowledgments

My crew; Betas and ARC team you are all incredible! Thank you for reading, reviewing and sharing all my books. I am so grateful to you all.

Heatwave brings the International Love series to a close. It has been an incredible ride with these characters and I'm so honored to have been able to share them with you.

Cheryl's Literary Corner, your editing has been spot on. Thank you for your amazing attention to detail!

Remember readers…rules are made to be broken and steamy truths are a way of life.

Cassidy xo

CASSIDY LONDON

About the Author

Cassidy London has been in love with books ever since she can remember; particularly, scandalous steamy romances. When she's not writing or reading dirty books, Cassidy can also be found masquerading as a wine drinking, suburban mom, in Montreal, Canada.

CASSIDY LONDON